Big book

Straight to gay erotica

Kyle Rayne

EXPERIMENTAL FIRST TIME

Straight to gay erotica

Kyle Rayne

I 've been single for longer than I'd like to admit. I blame it on being in college which is the opposite of what most men think. According to their fantasy, women are supposed to fall at our feet like ripe pears. I am a football quarter back...there are cheerleaders.

Problem is me I guess, not them. I don't find any of them attractive. I don't know if it's the color of their hair, or the size of the tits. Nothing about them turns me on. It's supposed to, isn't it? I'm supposed to think about their plump tits in the shower when I jerk-off? Well, since I'm being honest...I don't fantasize about women.

"Cameron, are you alright?" Jason, my dormmate asked me.

"I'm fine."

But I wasn't fine. If there was one person I'm attracted too, it's him, not the cheerleaders. I've known I had a crush on him longer than I'd like to admit.

I closed my text book and shoved it in my backpack. I laid back on my shitty little bed... the bed that's too close to Jason. He jacks off when he thinks I'm sleeping and I can hear everything. I can hear the wet sounds of the lube when he slides up and down his length. I can hear the rustling of the bedsheets. The worst part is when he cums, he doesn't try to be quiet. He's a moaner and it always makes my dick hard.

Jason sat down on my bed. This was the first time he's done this.

"I know when something's bothering you, man."

He's not helping the situation, he's making it worse. He smells so fucking nice! He's freshly shaven and smells like aftershave. I love masculine-smelling shit...on men. He shouldn't make my dick start to trickle up with blood, but he does. I took a deep breath and put a pillow over my semi erect dick.

"Ok, you caught me."

"So, are you going to tell me?" He looked away and crossed his arms. "It's probably none of my business anyway. It's probably about a girl."

He stood up and I grabbed his wrist. Well, I guess I'd better come out with it then.

"It's not about a girl. It's about you," I choked out. He looked at me with curious eyes.

"Really?" he asked.

"Yes, really." I ran my hands through the scruff on my face. "When I look at women, it doesn't do anything for me. But when I look at you..." My voice was hoarse and gruff. "At least can we...kiss? Just to see if we like it?"

"I'm not gay."

"It's ok, me neither. We don't have to slap a label on it. We are just two consensual adults who are going to kiss, ok?"

I've seen him shirtless plenty of times. His body is more ripped than mine. It's because he's a swimmer.

He sat down on the bed and it creaked under the weight of us.

"Just a kiss," he rasped.

I pulled my shirt off because, fuck, I wanted the skin to skin contact. "Shirt off," I told him.

"Good idea."

He peeled his shirt off and tossed it on his bed. The only thing he had on were his thin gray sweatpants. He was always free-balling under them. They were so thin I could always see his dick-print. I groaned when he laid down next to me. My heart was hammering out of my chest when he looked at me with lustful intentions. I didn't want to be rude, so when he pressed his mouth to mine, I closed my eyes.

Oh God... I knew he would taste amazing.

Fuck, kissing him felt so good. More than good actually. He was a fucking phenomenal kisser! His tongue flicked around my mouth and the way he was moving his head around... My dick was pumping up with blood. His body was pressed against mine and I wanted more. I moaned, I couldn't help it.

My dick went ramrod straight, unlike me, I joked to myself.

He broke our kiss. "Cameron, your dick is pressed against my thigh." I had thick jeans on but I knew he would still feel it. I suddenly wished I had something as thin as his sweats.

"Want to touch it?" I rubbed my hips on his legs and he bucked back.

"No, I told you already I'm not-"

"Gay," I finished for him. I ran my hands down the ripples of his abs to his thighs. His dick was tenting his sweats. "Looks like your body says differently."

Jason groaned as I caressed his body, his eyes lidded heavily with lust. "If it feels good, it's ok, right?" he asked me.

"As long as we are two consenting adults, there's no reason we shouldn't be able to have sex," I told Jason. His eyebrows were scrunched in thought. I started to unzip my jeans and shimmy them off.

"Wait man, I didn't say 'yes' yet."

"I'm just getting comfortable. My boner was caught in a weird angle in my jeans and it was painful. You've seen me in my boxers before, haven't you?"

His cheeks flushed with a dark shade of red. "Yes."

"So, it's not a big deal. Do you want to kiss me again?" I was painfully hard—my nuts were aching.

"I need to come. If you decide you don't want to fool around, it's alright. I'll just head to the shower and rub one out. Let's just kiss and touch. Where this goes is up to you," I said.

"Fuck man, you make it sound like you'd suck my dick," Jason choked out.

"Can I?" I cocked my eyebrows in question. I never knew this deep hidden part of myself before. My carnal desires were locked away and hidden for so long.

"Kiss me first and I'll think about it."

"Whatever you want baby."

We were kissing and our bodies were pressed together. I loved that we were shirtless but I wanted the fucking boxers gone. Jason was so turned on that he was dry humping my abs and I could see the wet spot on the thin fabric. He was leaking copious amounts of precum. I pulled away from our kiss and his expression was lust-dazed expression.

"Babe," I rasped, "You're miserably hard. Let me take care of you. I'll make you feel so good—I promise."

I wanted to suck all of his juices clean out of him. I was trying to be a respectful lover and not just rip his pants off. I was feeling crazy, like I might do it. I couldn't do that to him, or anyone. That wasn't me. Jason didn't answer me so I got up off the bed and put my jeans back on. I needed to jack off. I needed to get out of here before I did something I wouldn't forgive myself for.

I shouldn't have expected him to want me the same way. He clearly told me he wasn't into me or men in general.

I was nearly out the door when he called out, "Wait, where are you going?"

"To masturbate in the shower."

"Don't go. I want you. Please Cameron," his voice was ragged and gruff. I loved his deep voice. "It's just... I've never done this before. I've suspected for a long time that I was..."

"You don't need to say it, unless you are ready to come out, Jason."

"I'm gay, ok?" he huffed out. It looked like a huge weight was lifted off his shoulders.

"Do you feel better for saying it?" I asked.

Jason smiled at me coyly. "I do. But I'll feel even better when you suck me off."

"I need to say it out loud for the first time ever. I'm gay."

"Now that we've got that out of the way, let's pick up where we left off," Jason said. We were both filled with newfound confidence.

He pulled his sweatpants down and his hard cock smacked his stomach with a thud. I dropped to my knees in front of the bed. His cock was beautiful. It was lengthy and slender. His veins and cock head were flushed purple with blood. His delicious cock head that was wet...so wet and juicy.

I licked his wet slit and teased it open. I sucked his slit, desperate for his salty precum. The way he bucked his hips and gripped the bed sheets told me how much he was liking this.

"F-fuck, that feels good," he choked out.

"I've never had anyone do it to me, although sometimes I play with my slit. I use the pad of my thumb. I like the sensation. But that's enough talking."

I sucked him into my mouth and I loved the way he moaned. I was desperate to get his entire length down my throat. I've never done this before, but I've watched enough gay porn to know that you just need to relax and straighten your neck so your throat opens up.

"Oh Cameron!" he moaned and grasped fistfuls of my hair.

Even if I couldn't properly deep-throat him yet, I knew I would make him cum. I cupped his sac which was tight and close to his body. His balls were dusted with dark hair and fuck, I loved how his sac felt in my hands, they seemed to fit in my palm perfectly.

I loved everything about a man's body...but not a womans. That much was obvious as I slid a finger behind his balls and grazed his taint, then further down to his puckering hole.

"Oh fuck, I never knew that delt so good down there," Jason rasped. I figured it was safe to test the waters. I pressed my finger into him, just inserting it slightly.

"Wow, that feels amazing." I kept sucking his dick. Now that it was in my mouth, I never wanted to spit it out. It's like his length was designed to live in my mouth.

I looked up at him with a questioning glance and pushed my finger deeper in his warm, tight void. I was one knuckle deep. To my surprise, he grabbed my wrist and pushed my finger all the way in himself!

"I've fantasized about this for so long!" he moaned. He held my wrist there, grinding himself on my finger. I loved the way his hips jerked around. It was like he was moving my finger around, trying to place it somewhere. My finger grazed over a spot inside him and he nearly jumped off the bed.

"That's it! That's my prostate...Fuck Cameron. I'm going to-"

Hot ropes of cum started shooting down the back of my throat. It was delicious. It was salty, in a sweet kind of way. I loved the taste of him. I've tasted my own jiz, because I wanted to know what a man tasted like. But my flavor was distinctly different than Cameron. I knew I was going to be addicted to sucking his dick. I would suck him off every day for the rest of my life if he let me...

"Oh Cameron!"

I also loved watching his stomach and hip muscles flex when he orgasmed. I knew it would be hot, watching him unravel.

His dick was going soft and he pulled it out of my mouth. "I'm done and sucked dry."

"Good," I teased.

I stood up and took my jeans and boxers off and lazily stroked my dick. "If you don't feel comfortable to touch me, it's ok. I'll stroke my length and you can watch. We'll wait until you are more comfortable."

"No, I want to do it." I was delightfully surprised by his quick answer. He must have been dreaming about this moment as long as me.

He wrapped his strong calloused fingers around my length. He slid his fist up and down my shaft. I loved watching my dick appear and disappear in and out of his fist. I didn't know if he was going to give me a blow job. But it didn't matter though. When he was comfortable enough, he would touch my cock. I knew this wouldn't be the only time we fooled around.

"Fuck babe, I'm going to cum," I rasped. I could already tell he liked the nickname. When he started playing with by balls, I burst. I knew I wasn't going to last long.

He dove down and swallowed my crown into his mouth, swallowing most of my load. "F-fuck Jason!" I moaned.

He looked up at me and licked his lips. "Wow, you taste so good." I pulled him close to lay down next to me.

"You taste good too."

I had to kiss him again. I wanted a mixture of our tastes in my mouth. It was the most erotic and dirty thing... The taste of my jiz and his. Jason's dick was twitching to life again. I couldn't believe it, considering I'd sucked him dry. I fisted his cock.

"Do you need to come again, baby?" His cheeks flushed red. "If we are going to be lovers and more, we need to learn to communicate our wants."

"It's just... Are you... Would you let me cum in your ass?"

"Yeah babe, of course."

My brain signaled my dick to get hard again and I was high on lust fog. I could never deny him anything and besides, I've wanted this for so long.

I turned around and got on all fours to put my ass in the air. Now, I was completely exposed to him. "Make love to my ass," I said like a needy bitch.

"Let me get my lube," he said. I stayed put with my ass in the air. I didn't want him to change his mind.

He squirted the cold liquid on my ass. He grasped my cheeks with his strong hands and spread me open even wider. When I felt his crown press at my tight ring of muscle, I nearly blew another load without even touching my dick. I hadn't known that was possible...

Inch by inch he sank into me until he was fully inside of me.

"I never thought we would do this. You are so tight and warm. You feel amazing. Fuck, it feels good for you, doesn't it?" he asked.

"Fuck yeah it does. Are you going to fuck me or just talk about it?"

He dragged his dick out and pushed it back in. "I'm going to fuck you now and every night until you don't want it anymore."

"I'll always want you..."

My mind was gone—I was moaning and biting the bedsheet. My dick was tangled in the blanket, but it didn't matter. I wasn't concerned about stroking my dick. I just wanted to enjoy my fucking.

I loved the obscenely loud sounds of our bodies smacking together. I was sure we'd break this cheap-ass bed. It was creaking and groaning. Our moans were loud as fuck. The headboard was tap, tap, tapping against the wall. It was absolutely the best music I've ever heard my life. There'd be no doubt that Jason was my boyfriend because everyone would hear him screaming my name any second now.

"Oh fuck, Cameron!" he screamed. It was so loud, I'm sure the whole dorm heard it.

Hot ropes of cum pumped deep inside of my ass. It felt good, better than I imagined. The pleasure of the wet warmth set off a reaction inside of me. My dick was shooting a load into the bedsheets.

"I'm coming babe, so fucking hard!"

After I came, we collapsed and cuddled. It felt right, like this was where we were supposed to be.

"This wasn't a onetime thing, was it?" Jason asked me.

"No babe, this was just the beginning." I traced my fingers through his chest hair. "We can do this in secret, or we can be open about it. I'm not ashamed of my sexuality. Are you?"

He was frozen in thought. My heart was hurting, just thinking about what he would say. I wanted just more than sex from him.

"I don't want to pressure you and push you away. Let's just sleep on it, ok?" I said.

"No, I want a relationship, if that's what this is. Can it be?" he shyly asked.

"Yes, of course it can." I trailed kisses down his neck to his taut chest.

"But I still need to shower," I told Jason. "Care to join me?"

"Yeah, let's go."

Our small dormitory had communal showers. Each dorm had a half bath, but if you wanted to shower, you had to venture to the next building over.

I was curious how Jason would act as soon as we left the room. I wanted to show the world how much I cared about him. What we did was so intimate...

To my surprise, he interlaced our fingers as we walked. Most people didn't give a shit these days if you were gay. But there are those who glowered at us like we were crazy.

"Fuck them," I whispered. "Don't feel insecure, not now. Are you ok?"

"I'm fine," he proudly said.

We were almost to the showers when I heard some call out. "Jason!" I turned around and peeked over my shoulder. It was my football coach.

"It's about fucking time you two got together. I was wondering if you guys would ever figure it out."

"You mean... you knew?" Jason asked.

Coach rolled his eyes. "Everyone knew, except you." He clapped me on the back. "Congratulations, finally."

We got to the showers and got into the same stall.

"Let them look," I said, "they are just jealous." There were only a couple guys here, just freshmen. As long as we were together, it didn't matter what anyone else thought.

"Let me wash you," I said. I wanted to learn every curve and crevice of his body. I couldn't get enough of him. I explored his body with my palm and a bar of soap. I got to see him naked in all his glory.

"Your turn," he said and grabbed the soap.

This was just the beginning for us, I couldn't wait to see what this led too.

Jason

I woke up with Cameron cuddled next to me. My morning erection was already tenting the sheets. He groaned as he woke up and I grinded my hips, into his.

"Hey baby," he sweetly said. It fucking melted my heart when he called me babe or baby. I never had a girlfriend be so sweet with me. I know Cameron is my boyfriend, but you get the point.

I stuck my hand into his boxers and fisted his cock. "There's something I've always wanted to try."

"Yeah? What's that?" His voice was deep and seductive.

We took our boxers off and threw them to the side. I grabbed the bottle of lube from the nightstand and squirted a liberal amount in my fist.

"Get on top of me and press your balls to mine."

"Shit, ok."

Cameron was right where I wanted him. His cock was dangling over mine, the tip red and flushed with blood. Both of our slits were leaking precum. I grabbed our dicks and pressed them together with both of my hands.

"Fuck my hands."

Our hips thrust together, the slick sides our dicks rubbing each other. I loved the wet sounds of my hands on our cocks as we thrust in and out. It was obscenely loud and I fucking loved it.

It didn't take long, Cameron was spilling his load all over my stomach. It was so warm and wet and just hearing him rasp my name pushed me over the edge. My dick shot jiz on my stomach, I was doubly coated. I'd always known two dicks would be better than one.

Two years later

"Happy anniversary," Cameron told me and kissed my neck. "I love you babe."

"I love you too." It still melted my heart when he called me babe.

The End

DOUBLE DIP

Straight To Gay

Kyle Rayne

I just got home from my shift at the restaurant. I walked into the kitchen and saw two bowls on the counter—one had chips, the other had salsa. This was my roommate's favorite snack. I always wondered how he kept his washboard abs even though he ate so much crap. He was a lifeguard, so I guess he had to be in shape. Me? I'm a waiter. It's nothing glorious but it pays the bills. As for my body, I suppose I'm a little huskier.

I usually didn't eat his food, but fuck it. He left it here and he wasn't home...I started munching away not caring about double-dipping, which was a major pet peeve of his. The crunching of chips was so loud in my ears that I didn't hear Eric come into the kitchen.

"Hey Gabe, helping yourself I see." His hands were on his hips and he wore nothing except plaid boxers. My eyes darted right to his junk because that's where the V carved on his hips led me. The button was undone and I could see through the slit. I saw his balls, lightly dusted with dark hair and when he strode closer to me, I saw the head of his dick...Fuck, I nearly groaned out loud. That's not me though—I'm a straight man. I've never looked at guys sexually before.

Eric opened the bag of chips and poured more in the bowl and that's when I saw another man walk into the kitchen. He was wearing just black boxer briefs. I saw his dick-print and the bulge of his balls through the thin tight fabric, so I looked down. I could see the tan lines of swim trunks on his muscular legs. He must have been a lifeguard like Eric. I suddenly felt like a dick. This was their food and I was the third wheel. It was obvious they just had sex and were having an after-bang snack. Even I knew sex burned lots of calories. They obviously had sex-hair, which was rumpled and disheveled on both of them. But seeing two men nearly naked... It was messing with my mind. It looked so erotic. Fuck, what was wrong with me?

Eric's houseguest wrapped his arms around his waist and started kissing him. I blushed and looked away, covering my eyes with my hand.

"Sorry, I didn't know you had company tonight." I walked out of the kitchen with my hand covering my eyes. "I'll just go out to dinner to give you guys some privacy." Our apartment walls were thin and I didn't want to hear them fucking. *At least someone's getting laid tonight.*

They kept kissing at fuck, it was making my dick hard. I was trying not to watch them when I was tying my shoes. I felt my cheeks flushing, along with my dick. If I didn't get out of the apartment soon, they were going to fuck whether I was there or not. When I saw Eric's hands cup his friends ass, pulling his hips closer, I audibly choked out.

"F-fuck. You guys are wild."

Eric looked over at me. "My roommate Gabe, I told you he was shy and cute."

"You're right, he is cute," Eric's friend coquettishly said.

"Me...cute?" I knew I was shy.

Eric locked eyes with me. "I already told you, Brady, he wouldn't want to join us." I suddenly realized he was flirting with me, even though he already had company... I felt my cheeks flush red. I dropped my keys and phone.

"Join you guys? What exactly would we do?" My voice sounded like I'd been eating gravel. I couldn't deny that I was...curious. I'd never had a threesome before. I definitely was never with a man before. Maybe, just maybe I wanted too. I didn't think it was wrong

19

to be curious.

These two muscle-clad hunks were looking at me with lustful eyes. I was in good shape, but not like them. Eric strode over to me with an obvious tent in his boxers. He ran his fingers through my scruff. "I love it when you forget to shave. I bet that'd feel good on my balls. Or Brady's."

My chest was tight because I was nervous but my dick was pumping up with blood. I was almost fully erect and my boner was caught in an awkward angle in my boxers.

"Let's make him feel good first," Brady said, "then we'll see if he wants to return the favor."

Before I knew it, they were both standing in front of me, practically naked.

"Do you want us to make you feel good?" Eric asked. Dammit, all the blood was gone from my brain because it was in my dick. I was dizzy with lust.

"I'm not really a hit-and-run type of guy."

"This doesn't have to be a onetime thing," Brady told me, "Eric has had a crush on you for a long time."

Eric said, "It will be just the three of us until we don't want it anymore. Does that sound good?" It did sound good. My dick wanted out of my pants to play. "F-fuck, okay." They both dropped to their knees and were clawing at my pants. My pants hit the ground and my dick sprang free, smacking Eric in the face with a *thud.*

"Look how hard you are," Eric said and fisted my cock. My knees nearly buckled. "Your dick looks as good as I'd fantasized." He dragged his tongue over my leaking slit and my legs were shaking.

Brady chuckled, "let's go to the bed before he falls down."

I was naked and in Eric's bed. Fuck, it smelled like him and Brady. Eric climbed between my legs and his balls were touching mine, his cock jutting up like an iron bar. His hands rested on my knees, spreading them obscenely wide.

"Are you going to fuck me?" I asked with a hoarse voice. He slid his finger into my sensitive crack, my taboo void. I'd never been touched there, but the way he gently caressed it...Fuck it felt good.

"If you want to give me your virgin ass, I'll gladly take it. But first..." Before I could ask what that meant, he sucked me into his mouth. My hips bucked in response and I ran my fingers through his short hair.

"F-fuck," I choked out.

Brady chuckled and jerked his dick. "What until you see what he does next. Can I kiss you while he does it?" My chest heaved as I watched my dick appear and disappear into my roommate's mouth. I loved the obscenely wet slurping sounds as he sucked up and down my length. His mouth was so warm and wet, it was better than any pussy I've had. And the way he worked my cock head with is tongue, it was absolutely amazing.

"Yeah, let's kiss."

My entire dick was in Eric's mouth, my head sliding down his throat. I never knew a dick could go that deep. My new boyfriend loves deep-throating, hooray for me! Brady slid his tongue in my mouth and kissed me feverishly. I suddenly felt brave and reached down and grabbed his dick, he moaned into my mouth. I touched his dick the same way I liked to stroke mine. I never touched a dick other than mine before, but fuck, I liked it. I cupped his sac and played with his balls. Turns out I like that too. I especially loved the way Brady groaned while I was playing with him.

Eric sucked me deep until my head hit the back of his throat. I felt my nuts wrench up tight to my body, I was going to cum soon. I felt a finger teasing my hole and fuck, just the pressure of it there felt good. I broke the kiss between Brady and I.

"Stick a finger in me," I told Eric.

"Sure babe, just tell me what you want. I want to make you feel good."

He squirted lube on my hole and pushed a finger in.

"F-fuck," I choked out, "Two fingers, give me."

Brady chuckled. "You lost our bet Eric. I told you he'd be into ass-play." I was about to ask what the bet entailed, that was until I screamed. "Oh fuck!" Two big strong fingers slid inside of me. There was a spot inside me, a pleasure nub that felt good...so good. Eric kept fingering that special mysterious spot. I felt like my dick was getting stroked from the inside.

"How are you doing that?" I choked out.

"That's your prostate. I'm going to milk it, baby. Ok?"

I was so new to this and I didn't know what any of that meant. He sucked me deep and pressed that spot inside me just right. It was double the pleasure. I was feeling good inside and out. My groin felt like it was on fire! My balls exploded.

My dick started spurting a steady rope of cum down the back of Eric's throat. I was coming with a continuous rope of semen, not just the typical spurts. He drank me down.

"H-holy fuck!" I screamed.

I never knew there was so much cum in my dick and Eric sucked me completely dry. He kept sucking and I pulled my dick out of his mouth, I was so sensitive now that I was entirely empty. I was a boneless fucked-out mess.

"Wow," I rasped, "so that's what 'milking' meant."

Eric kissed me. "I'm glad you liked that."

"I more than liked it!" I noticed my new boyfriend's cocks were both hard. I was high on after-sex endorphins and I felt brave. "Let me suck you guys off." They both looked at me skeptically. "I want to do it." I really wanted to do it. I was suddenly cock-starved.

"Only if you're sure," Eric told me, "we didn't do this for a favor in return." He was lazily stroking his cock, precum beading out of the tip. It looked wet, juicy and delicious. I wanted to lick and suck Eric's fluids, and Brady's. I wanted to know what they tasted like,

I sat up on the edge of the bed and took a dick in each hand. Fuck this was hot, double jacking them off. They both started moaning as my hands slid up and down their length.

I had a hard time choosing whose dick to suck first. I guessed it didn't matter. I was going to give each cock equal attention, so it really didn't matter. "You first," I told Eric and Brady whimpered. It was cute. "Don't worry, I'm sucking both of you off. Eric is first because I've known him longer." I grabbed his cock and started to stroke it, and that quieted him up. Fuck, touching another man's cock...there was something so erotic about it. I had two beautifully hard dicks in front of my face to play with. So, play I shall.

I sucked Eric into my mouth and he tilted his head back and groaned.

"I've been dreaming of this forever, Gabe," Eric rasped as my mouth slid up and down his length. He ran his fingers through my sandy-blonde hair. I was sucking Eric and jerking off Brady. A cacophony of moans rang through the air. I felt so hot and desirable for the first time in my life. It was powerful! I had these muscle-clad men in the palm of my hand. Well, one in my hand and the other in my mouth. That reminded me, it was time to switch. I spit Eric's dick out. "It's your turn Brady."

"Oh yeah," Brady moaned, "Eric, kiss me while I get sucked off. You know I love that."

My mouth slid up and down his length and I stroked Eric. Brady tasted differently, but good. He tasted faintly of soap and his precum was rapidly leaking in my mouth. It was salty in a delicious way. I was becoming addicted to sucking dick when minutes ago, I'd never done it before. I loved the slurping sounds my mouth made. I moaned on his shaft because fuck, I was loving this!

"Oh baby!" Brady grasped my head from behind and he started pumping loads of cum in my mouth. I wasn't sure if I was going to swallow it, but I gulped it down.

I loved it! I loved the taste of another man's cum. I felt dirty for thinking that, but in the best way. I wasn't ashamed.

Eric started shooting his load on my face, I spit Brady's cock out and swallowed Eric's head in my mouth.

"F-fuck Gabe!" Eric shouted.

"Did you swallow it all?" Brady asked me. I chuckled, "isn't that what I was supposed to do? I'm super new to this, remember?"

"Next time, save some for me and we'll kiss to share it," Brady told me, "it's called 'snowballing." My cheeks flushed hot, "you guys are dirty. I've never heard that term before."

"There's probably another term you should know," Eric told me, "I'm a 'power-bottom."

Brady cut in, "it means he loves to take bottom."

"What?" I rubbed the scruff nervously.

"I love to get fucked in the ass," Eric said with a husky flirtatious chuckle.

I realized what that meant. He wanted me to fuck him…This morning when I woke up, as far as I knew, I was a perfectly straight man. Now, I'll be participating in anal sex! I laid back and yawned. "You guys are on your own tonight."

"Tomorrow then?" Eric asked me.

"Sure." I got up to leave Eric's room.

"Wait," he called out, "aren't you going to sleep in the bed with us tonight?"

After what we did, it felt so natural to want to sleep with both of them. It was so intimate what all three of us did. They both looked at me with longing. I strode to the bed and climbed in the middle of them. They nuzzled me and wrapped me up in limbs. I think I fell asleep in minutes.

I woke up to two meaty dicks pressed at my sides. Before I knew it, we were all moaning and kissing. I took a dick in each hand. I felt so powerful because they mewled under my touch.

"I'm going to suck you both first before I bury my cock in Eric. But now that we're swapping spit and cum, I don't want to hear about double dipping the chips. I'm double dipping dicks!"

Eric let out a throaty laugh. "Ok, no problem."

I sucked Eric first, then Brady. I paid careful attention to give each cock equal attention. Both of their dicks tasted like sex from last night. The dirty taste made it all the more sexy. And the smell of them both...Fuck, they both smelled like sex and I loved it. I really didn't know why I thought it was so hot.

Brady pumped hot ropes of cum in my mouth. I kept it in my mouth but I didn't swallow it. I kissed Eric and sucked my mouth dry.

"I didn't cum yet," Eric told me, "I think you know what I'm waiting for."

"Yes sir," I chuckled.

Eric flipped over on all fours and put his ass high in the air. "I'm going to ignore that you called me 'sir." Brady squirted lube on Eric's hole and tossed me a condom. "You don't need to prep him since I fucked him yesterday." I groaned as I rolled the condom down my length. "Oh f-fuck," I moaned, just looking at his puckering hole. I ran my hands down the globes of his hairless ass. I gripped his hips and thrust my hips to put my head at his opening. His pink ring of muscle was puckering.

"Fuck me, please," Eric begged.

I pushed my head in and the muscle sucked me in deeper...and deeper. It was like his internal walls sucked me in until I was balls-deep.

"You're so tight," I rasped. I dragged my dick in and out of his tight channel. "Your dick, it's so thick," he rasped.

I stopped. "I don't want to hurt you."

Brady was laying on the bed, enjoying the show. "He loves it, trust me."

Eric groaned. "He's right, please don't stop fucking me."

"That's all I needed to hear." I pounded my dick in his ass and my nuts were so tight, it was nearly painful.

"I'm going to cum," I rasped. I dug my hands into his ass and my balls started pumping ropes of cum into the condom barrier, but fuck, it still felt good.

"Oh Eric!" I rasped.

I collapsed, I was a boneless fucked-out mess again.

Brady slid a finger in between my cheeks and caressed my hole.

"I need to cleanup first," I chuckled. "At least we can all fit in the big walk-in shower. And for the record, I might drop the soap on purpose. You guys can take turns with me."

We all got in the shower. "Let us wash you," Brady rasped. Eric grabbed the bar of soap and lathered up my chest hair and the soap dripped down to my balls. Brady traced patterns in my hair that led from my navel to the root of my dick.

"I love this hair," Brady said, "my body hair never grew thick."

"I don't know what to say except I'm glad you guys are enjoying my body so much." I wasn't muscular like them and they didn't seem to mind.

I rinsed the soap of my body and bent over, exposing myself to them. "I want your dicks to touch that special spot inside of me. Please," I begged.

"Whatever you want baby," Eric groaned. "We'll take care of you and make you feel so good."

They took turns loving and worshipping my ass and I've never felt so good or sexy before. They said we could keep doing this until I wanted to stop, but I knew I never would want this to end.

The End

TRUTH OR DARE

Experimental first time

Kyle Rayne

I only came to this stupid party because my sister Jessie said I needed to get out of the house and socialize. It's not that I'm anti-social. I work and go to college which means I don't have lots of free time. I'm just busy.

I only came to make her happy. These are her friends, not mine. And not to mention, I'm just not nig on drinking. Well, I'm sipping my beer to help me loosen up.

"Alex, have fun and just chill out," Jessie said, "and don't act like a dork and embarrass me or I'll never invite you again."

"Whatever," I huffed out and walked away. She's always been my annoying younger sister. Super annoying, actually.

Looking around the crowd, there's your usual assortment of party shenanigans. I feel so… out of place.

"Oh hey Alex!" Brittany shouted and started to make way across the room.

"Shit," I muttered under my breath, she couldn't hear me over the loud music. I started to drink my beer quicker than I intended.

She was standing in front of me with a huge grin. *Fucking god dammit.* I wasn't attracted to her. I don't know why. She has big tits and blonde hair. Maybe it's her personality?

She playfully swatted at my chest. "I see your sister dragged you out of your apartment."

What was she expecting me to say? I was so awkward in social situations like these.

"Sure did." A loud song came on—a popular song I recognized. She grabbed my free hand.

"Come on, let's dance." Brittany started to pull me away towards the living room. Could this night get any worse?

"Hold on Brittany," a deep voice purred, "Alex and I are going to study for the big exam. Aren't we?" It was Jake. He looked at me with a calm expression. We weren't necessarily friends. We had a few classes together... with Brittany.

"There's no exams coming up," Brittany said and nursed her fruity drink. I was frozen with my social anxiety.

"It's an extra credit assignment. Come on Alex, let's go," Jake said.

"Yep, we gotta study," I replied. I yanked my hand out of Brittany's little wrist.

"You guys are no fun," she protested with a pouty face.

Jake and I left the apartment with our beers. I felt so relieved when the door closed behind me.

I took another drink. "Thanks for saving me back there."

The way Jake was looking at me... it was intense. His eyes were dark, along with his short hair. His face was dusted with scruff. I think he shaved only once a week or so, but he pulled off the look well.

"I could just tell you weren't interested. It was obvious to anyone looking. She was making you uncomfortable."

"It was obvious to anyone except her."

"Let me walk you home," he said. The apartment hallways were empty except for us.

"It's alright. My apartment is only one floor down and I'm sure you want to go back to the party."

"I actually don't. I'll walk with you."

We took the elevator down one level. My apartment was the first on the left once you left the elevator. I fumbled with my keys once I got them out of my pocket. The way Jake was looking at me... In the dim light, I noticed how defined his facial features were and how the hair accentuated those features. He was taller than me, although not by much. I fumbled my key into the lock and opened the door.

"Well Alex," he rasped deeply, "Aren't you going to invite me in?"

I froze again. But this was different than with Brittany. I didn't want her company.

"Yeah, sure, come in," I managed to say.

He reached out and placed a hand on my shoulder. "You don't need to be nervous with me."

"Sure." I closed the door behind us and locked it. I didn't want my dorky sister interrupting whatever *this* was.

I threw my empty bottle in the trash. "So, what do you want to do, since we aren't going to study?"

He ran his fingers through his scruff. "Let's play truth or dare."

I choked out laughing. "Ok then." It seemed so juvenile and

immature, but I couldn't deny that I was… curious.

I sat down on the couch and patted the seat next to me. I didn't usually drink, so one beer in my system gave me liquid courage. It was weird though, I cringed when Brittany touched me, but not when Jake did. When he put his hand on my shoulder moments ago, I wanted him to touch me *more*.

He plopped down unceremoniously next to me with a mischievous grin.

"Truth or dare," he said with a smirk.

"Truth." I wiped my sweaty palms on my pants.

"Good choice, it's usually so hard to get you to talk. So, tell me Alex. How many women have you slept with?"

Fuck. Why did he have to ask me that? I was a virgin and what makes it worse is that I'm a college student. I should have been laid ten times over.

"Two… I've fucked two chicks." I knew I sounded like an idiot. "Your turn Jake."

"I pick truth," he said with a sly grin. Was he doing this just to get me out of my shell?

"Alright Jake, how many women have you been with?"

He balled his fist and put it under his chin. With a huge grin, he said, "None."

"You're a virgin?" I choked out.

He put his other hand down next to my thigh, but his eyes were locked on mine. "I'm not a virgin. I've had two lovers, unlike you. I know you aren't being truthful with me."

I felt blood start rushing to my dick. The way he was looking at me, yet he knew I lied. My mind was putting the pieces together... He had sex with two men. My chest was heaving just imagining it.

"Truth or dare, Alex," he purred. His hand was resting against my thigh now.

"Dare."

He leaned forward, his lips were an inch from mine. "I dare you to kiss me." Fuck, I could feel his breath on my lips. I could smell his cologne and a faint scent of liquor on his lips. He coyly licked his lips and I lost it. It was so fucking erotic... I was imagining that tongue licking my balls like that. I was freshly shaven and I wanted to feel his scruff on my smooth skin.

"Is this about the game, or do you really want to kiss me?" I asked.

He wrapped his arms around my neck. Just that small touch was making my dick hard.

"I've liked you for a while now Alex. You just didn't notice."

I was shocked and didn't know what to say, kiss it is then. I got brave and put my hands on his thighs.

"Just a kiss," I rasped. Before I could change my mind, I pressed my face into his. Our lips touched and he groaned. The sexual ravenous sounds escaping him as my tongue slid in my mouth made my dick an iron rod.

His tongue flicked around my mouth, swirling with his. I

never knew kissing would feel so *good*. My dick was nearly fully erect and it was caught in a weird angle in my boxers. My hands were on my lap, so I quickly adjusted my boner.

I pulled away from our kiss. It felt good and I didn't want to stop, but...

"I dare you to take your shirt off," I said with a deep husky voice.

"I didn't pick dare," he said while peeling his black t-shirt off, "but it doesn't matter." He threw his shirt behind him. "Dare done."

Oh gawd, his body was nice. He had hard muscular pecs and abs that rippled around his core. I didn't have a body like that...

His chest was dusted with dark hair and it was particularly thick under his navel where it trailed beneath his jeans. I nearly groaned out loud, imagining what else was dusted with dark hair. My body hair didn't grow thick like that. Sure it was there, but not like his. I wanted to run my fingers through it.

"Like what you see?" he asked with a deep raspy voice.

"I do." I didn't see the point in lying.

He slid a hand up my t-shirt sleeve. "Take this off."

I took my shirt off and now here we were... both shirtless. I knew I had an erection. I looked at the bulge between his legs, he had a boner, like me.

"Game's over," he rasped, "but we both know we want to kiss again."

"Alright."

He reached out and stroked my chest. "I know you want this as much as me." Jake was right, I leaned in and kissed him. I let my hands rest on his thighs, and as we kissed, I moved my hands up his stomach and chest. He was letting me explore his body while we kissed. But fuck, my dick was hard and I wanted his body pressed against mine.

I got brave and straddled his lap while kissing him the entire time. I had to adjust my dick again. Jake pulled away from my mouth and kissed my neck and worked his way down my chest. I knew I was groaning. At this point, I was beyond turned on.

"I want to make you feel good," Jake purred. He stuck a finger down my pants and teased my hips. "Let me take care of you."

My heart was beating fast and my dick was hard... so hard. I wanted this, whatever *this* was. And suddenly it hit me like a ton of bricks. There's a reason I was a virgin. It's the same reason that I wasn't attracted to Brittany.

"Let's do this," I rasped, "I want you." I moved off his lap and fell to my knees. It was an accident because I was a little tipsy from the beer.

Fuck it. I wanted this...

I started to unbutton his jeans, my fingers were trembling when I unzipped his pants.

"Damn," he rasped, "if I didn't know better, I'd say your cock starved."

"I'm a virgin." I looked at the bulge underneath his tight black briefs.

"Oh fuck, man, I didn't know." He put his hands over his junk, hiding what I wanted to see very much.

"I want this. I want you," my voice was needy and sounded like I'd been eating gravel.

"I shouldn't have fooled around with you." His jeans were open and everything I wanted was right in front of me.

"Hey," I barked back, "I might not be qualified as experienced in the dick sucking department, but let me try."

"Only if you're sure." He moved his hands away. His dick was hard like mine. I put my hands in his boxer briefs and pulled them down.

"Oh fuck, look at that dick," I moaned.

It was lengthy and stood ramrod straight. It was corded with thick veins. I cupped his heavy sac then wrapped my hand around his shaft. His hips jerked and that's when I swallowed his head and took his length in my mouth. Fuck, his dick was long. I stroked him up and down as I sucked him.

"Damn, that's good. Fuck, you've never done this before?" he asked and ran his fingers through my short hair, tousling it.

I just moaned on his shaft in response. I hoped he knew I meant 'no.' I wasn't going to spit his dick out to tell him.

I loved the taste of his precum that was dripping in my mouth. It was salty and savory. I knew I was going to become addicted to his taste.

I slid my mouth up and down his length and jerked him at

the same time. With my free hand, I cupped his sac and it was tight and drawn up to his body. I liked the feeling of the soft hair that tickled my hand. Why was that so hot?

He placed his legs over my shoulders and the position of his body sank his dick deeper in my throat.

My cock was achingly hard and I needed it out of my pants. I moved my hand away from his balls and undid my pants, my cock sprang free. I jerked it twice and that's when I felt his hips buck and his ass cheeks tightened.

"Fuck, that's so hot watching you touch your own dick," Jake rasped.

He started spurting ropes of cum down the back of my throat. Fuck, it tasted so good that I drank him down. Spurt after spurt filled my mouth and he moaned and cursed under his breath. I wasn't sure exactly what he said, but I think I heard "motherfucker" and "bastard" escape his lips.

I kept his dick in my mouth even though I knew his orgasm was over. I liked his taste and I just like having a dick in my mouth.

"Ok, that's enough," Jake said with a deep, husky voice. He pulled his flaccid dick out of my mouth.

He cupped my chin. "Ok baby, it's your turn. I've wanted this for a while."

"Ok then." How could I refuse an offer like that?

I stood up and my dick was jutting out from my jeans, fully erect. I had more girth, but less length. He unceremoniously spit in his hand and rubbed it up and down on my shaft. It was so fucking dirty, yet hot.

"Can you spit on my shaft?" I asked. I didn't know I was such a freak, but fuck it. Right now, I had no shame. I was going to enjoy my first gay experience to the max, no matter how nasty it was.

"Yeah, I can." He moistened my shaft with his warm spit.

"There, that's better," he purred, "your nice thick dick is wet for me." His strong calloused hand wrapped around my girth and stroked me. My knees buckled, especially when he was playing with my nuts. He had my sac in the palm of his hand and rolled them around, massaging them. It felt good. I'd never touched my balls like *that* before.

"Oh fuck," I rasped as I watched my dick head disappear in and out of his fist. His hand was so strong, yet gentle. He was putting just the right amount of pressure around my length. Only a man would know how it feels when you stroke it that way. Not too rough, and not too soft either. His hand was perfect.

"Sit down and I'll take care of you," Jake said while pointing at the couch.

"Fuck, ok."

I kicked my shoes off and shoved my pants all the way off. I plopped down on the couch. My dick was leaking a copious amount of precum on my stomach, wetting my happy-trail. He dropped to his knees and lapped his tongue at my slit.

"That's good," I rasped.

"I wanted to taste you first before I suck you." He then flicked his tongue at the underside of my dick's head, the little V that's so sensitive. My hips bucked in response. I bet he knew lots of erogenous zones I never knew I had.

"Holy f-fuck dude," I rasped because I didn't know what else to say.

"Open your legs for me." He peeked up at me with such a coy, erotic gaze. I did what he asked, my heart pounding in anticipation. He slung my left leg over the crook of his elbow, splaying me open wide.

The next thing I knew, his warm mouth was swallowing my *entire* length. Holy fuck, he was deep throating me. My crown was bouncing off the back of his throat and when he took a breath, it went *deeper inside.*

I wasn't going to last long. My nuts were tingling, drawn up tight to my body. I could nearly feel my load about to shoot out. Dammit, I was trying not to cum so quickly. I'm not going to lie, watching a dude suck my dick was the *hottest* thing I've ever seen in my life. In a vivid moment of clarity, I can't believe I ever thought that I was straight. I fucking loved the way that the casual-looking scruff tickled my balls and length. Men and women were just so different... But I knew which one I preferred now.

"Jake, I'm gonna cum." He started moaning on my dick and the sensation reverberated my entire length. That was it for me.

My dick fired off, from my nuts and out of my shaft, deep down into Jake's throat. Spurt after spurt he sucked out of me.

He sucked me completely dry. It was the most intense orgasm of my life. He trailed kisses down my thigh to the crook of my knees.

I sat up and he stood up. We stood silently for a moment, looking at each other. I leaned forward and kissed him and wrapped my arms around his neck, our flaccid wet cocks were touching.

"Spend the night," I said with a tone needier than I intended. Jake kissed my neck and cupped my bare ass cheeks.

"Let's go to bed. Like I said before, I finally have you where I want you. You won't get rid of me so easily now."

I got a warm, wet wash cloth from the bathroom and wiped both of us off. I always liked cleaning myself after I jack-off. I don't know if other guys do it, but it's something I've always religiously done.

"Thanks," Jake chuckled.

"Come on, let's go to bed."

He climbed into bed next to me and I turned around so he could place his arm on me. I was the little spoon and I was cool with it.

The next morning, I felt something hard sliding between my cheeks. Of course I knew what it was. I didn't pull back though. I grabbed my cheek and pulled it open. I was surprised how *good* it felt back there. It was so sensitive in between my cheeks. Jake groaned in response, he was just waking up.

"Good morning baby," he rasped. I guessed *'baby'* was a thing now. I was cool with it. Actually, it tore me up inside in ways I didn't know were possible. Jake was completely undoing me.

He was kissing my back and up my neck. I broke out in gooseflesh when he kissed my neck at my hairline. I grinded my ass back on his length.

"Good morning to you too," I managed to say.

His cock head was pressed against my hole, because I grabbed his shaft and aligned it there.

"We don't need to do this now," Jake said, "You can jack me off instead."

I was fully intending on exploring what having sex with a man entailed. *All* of it. Even back *there*.

"I want it," I rasped and Jake let out a sultry chuckle.

"Ok, but I need to prep you first. I'll stretch you with my fingers."

"Oh," I shyly said. He had experience with this, whereas, I didn't know anything. "Let me get some lube."

His wet, slicked finger slid into my ass. I couldn't believe I was doing this. I was completely naked and exposed to Jake. But what I couldn't believe the most was that it felt *good*—amazing actually!

He pushed another finger inside and I grabbed his wrist to push him in deeper.

He chuckled. "Feels good. Doesn't it?"

"Fuck yeah," I choked out. "I'm ready. I want you inside of me Jake."

He climbed between my knees and slung my legs over the crooks of his elbows.

"Are you sure?" he asked.

"I'm sure. I need you inside me. Now," my voice was deep and gruff.

Just thrusting his hips, he aligned the crown of his head at my hole.

"It might sting when I push in. I'll go slow and it will fade," Jake explained.

He pushed in and it did sting, just slightly, but in a pleasurable way. He paused, I must have been scrunching my eyebrows.

"Keep going, just push in," I said. He slid slowly into me and fully bottomed out.

"I'll stay here for a minute, the sting will stop."

"It's gone, you can fuck me." He looked doubtful. "Please fuck me. Don't be a tease," I begged.

That was the only convincing that he needed. He was fucking me and we were moaning so loud, I'm sure the neighbors could hear it. I knew they would hear the headboard *tap, tap, tapping* on the wall. My head was bumping the headboard Jake was fucking me so hard and my feet were up in the air.

I jerked my dick once, twice and I was shooting all over my stomach.

"Fuck that's hot," Jake moaned and he started cuming deep... so deep in my ass. I felt spurt after spurt fill me up.

Once he pulled out, I was a boneless fucked out mess. It was a perfect place to be.

We got dressed and left my apartment. I invited him to breakfast. I was starving and didn't want to be a rude lover. I bet he was starving too. My heart neatly stopped beating when I saw my sister walking down the hallway with a shit-eating grin. Why do I feel like I just... got caught? We didn't do anything wrong. Jake firmly gripped the nape of my neck as my sister approached us.

"Baby," he purred, "Just be cool. Don't freak out."

"I'm freaking out."

Jessie stopped right in front of us with her hands on her hips and chewed her bubble gum obnoxiously.

"Aren't you glad I invited you to the party?"

"What?" I asked. "I mean, yes." I looked back at Jake.

She punched me in my shoulder. "You dork. I guess I knew before you."

"Whatever." I grabbed Jake's hand and interlaced our fingers. "Let's go. I don't need to be grilled by my little sister."

"Thank you!" Jake shouted back to Jessie.

"Your welcome!" she called back. It made me realize... She was in on the whole thing!

The end

KISS AND TELL

Experimental first time

Kyle Rayne

*R*ing, ring, ring.

I pulled my iPhone out of my pocket and saw my best friend Adam's ugly-ass mug pop up on screen.

"What?" I quipped. He was the only person I answered the phone like that. "What do you want?"

"Hey," he said in a mischievous voice, "So, I set you up on a blind date. This Friday night at our favorite Italian restaurant."

I ran my fingers through my hair and down the scruff on my face.

"No and no again. You aren't talking me into your bullshit shenanigans this time," I huffed out in annoyance. I didn't have time to... date. I was using air quotes in the air for my own dramatic purpose.

"Come on man. You've been alone for way too long and just because one relationship didn't work out, well, you don't deserve to be alone. No one does," Alex said.

We didn't usually talk about feelings and shit. It always made me uncomfortable, especially when past-feelings started churning in my belly. It made me uneasy and unsettled. Maybe that's why I've been alone for so long.

I could just go out for a fuck. That would have been fine, but that just wasn't me. Adam kept talking on and on. He was the chatty one, not me. "*Bla, bla, bla,*" he rambled on.

"Ok, Brody. You didn't answer me. Are you there?"

"Yeah, I'm here."

"You'll be there, Friday at six o'clock," he said and not asked.

"Whatever. I gotta go. I'm at work and my boss is looking at me with pissed-eyes." I hung up the phone and shoved it in my pocket. I was hiding in the backroom at work, so it's not like customers could see me.

Well, now it's Friday and I'm early at five thirty. It's a weird habit of mine—showing up early. I didn't like to be late anywhere I went and if you want a steady job these days, it's a good habit to have.

I hoped whoever she was wasn't the typical hipster who thought it was ok to show up an hour or more late. That's the thing about women. They take so long to get ready. Curling hair, putting on makeup and picking outfits. My ex always did that. She made us late anywhere we went if she wasn't happy with her lipstick choice or how a dress hung oddly on her hips.

I walked into the restaurant and was greeted by the hostess. I gave her the reservation information and she led me to the booth in the back. I always liked sitting back here. It was laid back, chill and private. I wondered if Adam requested this table. We've eaten here several times. It started out as double-dates. Then once I was single, I only came as the third wheel once.

I sat down on the left side of the booth and ordered a cocktail. Adam wouldn't tell me her name or what she looked like. It was a 'surprise.' I did tell him it was childish not to tell me...

I kept my eye on the door and watched every patron that came in. There were your typical groups and couples, no women. But a man came in that caught my eye. He was wearing a black button down shirt that wasn't buttoned to the top. His shirt was tucked into his jeans and he even had a nice belt on. His hair was brown and cropped short. He had a little scruff that was neatly trimmed around his masculine jawline. He looked... good?

I looked down at my hands—it was rude to stare. He was obviously in the same situation as me; waiting for our dates to arrive.

I looked at my watch, it was five fifty. She should be here soon, right? I was so nervous that I wasn't even hungry. I sipped my too sweet cocktail feeling better as the liquid courage was spreading in my gut.

I heard someone sit down on the squeaky booth and the leather made the familiar sounds under her weight. I looked up...

"I think you've got the wrong booth. I'm waiting for my date." It was the man in the black shirt. He didn't move an inch. Rather, his posture was so relaxed and casual.

"Hello Brody," he purred, "I am your date."

My hand jerked in shock and I spilled my drink. "What the fuck," I muttered under my breath. I was going to kick Adam's ass. I had a sudden urge to knock all of his teeth out of his skull. What the fuck was Adam thinking? That I was... I couldn't even say the word, not even to myself.

The man stood up and walked over to me and wiped the spilled liquor off my bare arms with a napkin.

"You poor thing," he said with a deep and husky voice, "You are completely flustered." He started wiping off my shirt with wet, soggy paper napkins and I felt my cheeks flush hot. Blood was roaring in my ears and my heart felt like it might explode. This day could not get any worse, until it did.

"You're soaked and sticky. Why don't we go back to my place and you can clean up. My apartment is five minutes from here."

I crossed my arms and didn't say anything. I was speechless.

"Look," he said and bent down slightly. "You are soaked. I can see your pants are clearly wet and probably your boxers too. Am I right?" His demeanor was so calm and it was oddly comforting. I lived an hour from this restaurant. I couldn't go home and clean up so easily. I was considering his offer. He was right, I was soaked, sticky and cold. It looked and felt like I pissed my pants. My dick was sticking to my balls because of the moisture. I *hated* that feeling.

"We can go back to my place. You can shower and I'll order pizza. I'll lend you some clothes while yours wash." He then looked me dead in the eyes. "We can just be two guys hanging out, nothing romantic, ok? We can watch the game on my big-screen TV." He pulled his keys out of his pocket. "I told Adam this was a bad idea."

I burst out laughing. "I'm going to kick his ass," I muttered.

"Me too, now let's go."

"Ok." I gave in. He said it was nothing romantic, so I didn't have anything to worry about.

Once we got in the car, I asked, "How do you know Adam?" The smell of leather 'new car smell' and cologne assaulted my nostrils but it was... nice.

"He's my cousin. Adam's always been the type of guy to meddle in people's personal lives ever since I can remember."

I huffed in amusement. "Sounds about right."

"For the record," he added, "this was purely his idea. Not mine."

"Oh, so you're not gay then?" I asked.

"I am very gay, Brody. But I don't know why he insisted on trying to set me up with an obviously very straight man. I tried telling him it didn't work like that."

This was so fucked up, I was laughing in hysterics.

"You didn't even tell me your name."

"Shane."

"Well, Shane. It's nice to meet you." I supposed I couldn't deny that it actually *was* nice hanging out with someone.

"Likewise," he calmly said and pulled his car into an apartment building parking-lot.

Once we were inside his apartment, he showed me to the bathroom. "Throw your dirty clothes outside of the door. Once you are in the shower, I'm only going to open the door and place a clean towel, shorts and a t-shirt on the counter. As you can see, I don't even need to come into the bathroom."

"Thanks." I stripped off my wet boozy-smelling clothes and balled them up. I made sure to wrap my t-shirt around my socks and boxers. It would feel so intimate to let him see my boxers. I knew he wasn't trying to push me into something he wanted. We were both victims of Adam's meddling.

I stepped into the shower once it was warm. I used his body wash and fuck, it smelt good. Too good, if you ask me. It was masculine and savory. I felt my mind wandering about what this would smell like on his freshly washed skin. My dick started to twitch.

'Oh no dick, no you don't. I'm not jerking you off in the shower of a gay man.' I felt like my dick was communicating back to me and saying, *'but he smells so nice!'*

'Fuck you dick.' I turned the water cold and doused my cock and balls as long as I could stand it. Yup, it shrunk right up; embarrassingly small, but who cares.

I pulled the shower curtain back and just like he said, there was a towel and clothes. Just a shirt and a pair of shorts, no boxers though. I came out of the shower and found Brody unbuttoning his shirt in the kitchen. I was watching him from behind. He peeled off his shirt to reveal a very chiseled body. I hadn't noticed before. *Wow.* He picked up a hangar off the kitchen table and put the shirt back on and smoothed out the fabric and put the hanger on the back of a chair. I was watching him do this small thing and it felt so intimate, like I shouldn't have been staring at him.

Shane sat down and took his socks and shoes off and his feet were very naked, like mine. Don't call me a freak, I didn't have a kink for feet. For me, being barefoot was something intimate, only done with lovers. I worked full time and closed-toe shoes were a requirement. It snowed often, so it's not like I even owned a pair of flip flops. I never left the house with exposed feet. But his feet were naked… in a non-fetishistic way, it was sexy.

Shane stood up and looked startled to see me standing there, gawking at him like a creeper. He was shirtless and the torso of that man! He looked like he was a carved statue.

"Oh, hey Brody. I didn't hear you come into the kitchen. I didn't loan you underwear. You're ok free-balling it for a while?"

"Yeah, I don't mind."

A knock on the door roused me from my thoughts—more accurately my drifting mind. *It is a nice body.*

"Pizza is here." He paid the delivery man and I realized this wasn't a date.

"Let me pay for half."

"If it will make you feel better, sure."

I handed him a twenty from my wallet. "I don't know if this is half, but is this good?"

He nodded and got two plates from the kitchen. He was still shirtless, just wearing jeans. He turned on the TV and the game was on. The TV was visible from the kitchen table, so that's where we ate.

Once we were finished Shane sat down on his couch. I noticed he was being very reserved, not overtly social or friendly. I knew he didn't want to make me uncomfortable. He silently watched the TV. As far as he knew, I just wanted to get my clothes clean and leave. Don't get me wrong, I did want to go home. Shane was very quiet and respectful while I felt my mind wandering. Maybe I did want to get to know him. He wasn't talking to me because… he wanted more 'than just a guy' to hang out with.

I sat down on the couch more closely than I knew was necessary—it was a big couch. Shane kept his gaze forward on the TV, not saying a word to me. His silence and respectfulness was intriguing to me. I had expected him to be pushy and aggressive. His calm energy was ensnaring me. His calm energy was so magnetic. He was a man that was just so comfortable in his own skin. He had himself figured out, whereas I didn't.

"So, how did you find out you were gay?"

Shane kept his eyes glued to the screen and clasped his hands behind his head.

"I was with a female once. I ate her out and finger-fucked her. My dick was lifeless and I didn't like it at all. I just didn't... I couldn't ever do it again. In life, I've learned there's just somethings that make people gag. For me, cunts and tits are one thing that set off my gag reflex. And the second thing is wet squishy coconut."

"Fair enough." I laughed and felt my cheeks turn red. Fuck, he was interesting.

"It could be a texture-thing. I don't like wet squishy consistencies. I can't stand wet coconut at the bottom of coconut water the same way I can't stand pussies."

"I don't like flan, so I know what you are talking about." For him it was purely a preference and I understood it. I respected it. And most of all... I was curiously intrigued by it...

I found myself scooting closer to him, desperate to see if he smelled like the soap in the shower. I inhaled and fuck, he did. I knew he smelt good back in the car. It was easier to inhale his scent in a small closed space.

I slid my bare foot closer to his, wondering what his feet would look like planted firmly into the mattress while his legs were spread open wide, dick jutting up in the air. My dick started twitching again and dammit, I didn't even have boxers, so I couldn't tuck it into the waistband. If I got any harder, I would be erect soon. And it was nothing more than my thoughts getting my dick hard.

Beep. "That's the washer," Shane said and stood up. "I'll throw your clothes in the dryer."

"Thanks."

He came back and sat further away from me and I didn't know why it bothered me so much. I stayed in the same spot, expecting him to sit next to me.

"Shane," I rasped. He looked over at me finally.

"Yes," he said with a silken voice.

He's going to think I'm crazy, but fuck it. "Will you sit next to me?" The look on his face was shocked, but pleased.

"Sure." He scooted closer to me and looked at the TV. I felt a stupid desperation to get his attention and cupped his chin, bringing his gaze to meet mine. He was still and silent like a statue.

"You're handsome," I blurted out before I could stop my brain.

"Oh?" he said in a drawn out questioning tone.

I felt my face flushing hot even though blood was trickling down to my dick.

"Would it be stupid if I asked... to kiss you. I know I ruined our date and I'm sorry. This is why I'm single. I'm just an awkward fucker. I-"

Shane cut me off with a gentle, "*Shush* baby, it's fine." He placed his hands on my chest. "You didn't ruin anything. I knew if you were comfortable, you'd ask me. I would never try to make someone do something they didn't want."

"You are so fucking nice and patient. You know that?" I rasped nervously.

"I'm a nurse. I'd better be patient."

"I'm a dick for not even asking you anything about yourself. I'll make it up to you. But... Can we kiss now and talk later?" I was desperate to feel what it was like to kiss Shane and to touch him.

He wrapped his arms around my neck. "Of course." He leaned forward and pressed his lips to mine. I pecked him a few times, just to feel him. I was testing the waters to see what it was like to kiss a man... I liked it. I more than liked it, actually.

I slid my tongue into his mouth and explored every inch of him. I loved the feel of his scruff on my face. Oh fuck, my dick was hard now—achingly hard. This was the most aggressive and passionate kiss of my life. Shane was one hell of a kisser. The way he moved his head from side to side. The way he gripped the nape of my neck. I wanted him to touch me below my shoulders, which he wasn't. I broke our kiss. I was out of breath like I ran a mile.

"Did you like that?" Shane asked.

"Fuck yeah I did," I rasped with a gravelly voice. "More than liked, actually."

He nipped playfully at my earlobe, then sucked it into his mouth. His tongue was so warm and wet. I knew it would feel good in other places.

"Oh my god," I moaned, "You are touching me in places that I never knew felt so good."

"A man's body is a wonderful thing to explore," he said this while looking into my eyes. I saw the invitation lingering there. I wanted this and I was never so sure of anything before. I pulled his wrists down and placed them on my thighs, close to my hips. What I wanted him to touch was right between his hands.

"We don't have to do this," he said with a kind smile. I felt like he was downplaying my wants. Like he was treating me so impersonally, which was fair because we didn't know each other. Just moments ago, I was telling him I was a straight man. I suppose I should appreciate him being cautious and not taking advantage of me.

"I don't want you to do something you'll regret," he finished.

This was my chance to back out, but I didn't want too. I didn't say anything. I grabbed his wrist and slid it over my dick.

"See how hard my dick is?" Please," I begged and looked down at my dick, now tenting the shorts. He rubbed my dick over the thin shorts and my breath hitched.

"Oh fuck your hard. So hard that it must be painful," Shane rasped.

I pulled the shorts down and my cock and balls popped out. It was a bold move, I know.

"That's a nice-looking cock," Shane teasingly said.

"Do you want to touch it?"

"I would love too." He wrapped his fist around my shaft and stroked me up and down.

"Oh fuck," I groaned and melted into his bare chest. I pulled him in for a kiss. It was a sloppy, wet and bruising-type kiss. I bit down on his bottom lip while he was stroking me.

"Take your pants off," I said, "You're nearly naked anyway. You've been showing off that rocking bod of yours."

"I'll give you whatever you want." He pulled down his zipper and his cock sprang out. It was thick and veiny.

"No boxers?" I laughed.

"Nope. Not when I'm at home but I wear them while I work."

Both of us had our pants on, just pulled down slightly. "I want these clothes out of the way," I said. We were kissing messily and ripping our clothes off. His hard dick was rubbing against mine. Our balls were touching and fuck, it felt good.

"Stay right here, I'm going to get us lube," Shane said.

He squirted the lube in his hands and rubbed it on my shaft then his. Our dicks were oiled up and slick. I didn't know what he was about to do. But whatever it was, I was sure he was going to blow my mind.

"Wrap your legs around my waist," he said.

"Ok," I said while my heart was hammering in my chest.

He stood between my legs, which were wrapped around his waist and he pressed our cocks together.

"This is one of my favorite positions," Shane told me. Before I could ask what he was doing, he wrapped his hands around both of our dicks.

"Thrust with me."

I wrapped my hands around his neck. I fucked his cock and his strong big hands. It was good… better than good. It was the best sex I've ever had. The slick sides of our cocks were grinding against each other, wrapped up in his hands. Together, we fucked his hands with our cocks. Up and down his hands glided on the wet, oily lube. I've never seen anything so sexy. I can't believe that I thought I was straight.

My nuts were hugged tight to my body and were tingling. I didn't want this to end, but I was going to cum.

"Fuck, Shane, I'm going to-" My load shot out, spurt after white milky spurt coated his crown and fists.

"Me too," he rasped and shot his load. My dick was going a little soft, but stayed erect enough when he shot his load and it sprayed all over my chest. He moved his hands away and I wanted more. I wasn't done. I sucked his dick right into my mouth. I needed to taste him, even if he couldn't cum again.

"You really don't have to," he rasped, so I reached up and stuck two fingers in his mouth to shut him up. Oh god, he tasted salty and musky in the best way possible.

His dick started to get hard again, I felt it pumping back up with blood. Up and down I sucked him like there was no tomorrow.

"Ung," he moaned when I cupped his sac. I wanted to explore every inch of his body. I had an urge to make him feel good while exploring my own sexuality. I slid two fingers under his balls and further down to his crack. It was warm and wet… so wet from our cum and dripping lube. I pushed a finger into his taboo crack and found what I was looking for. I put pressure on the tight ring of muscle.

"Oh baby," he rasped, "Don't tease me. Don't start what you don't intend to finish."

"I intend to finish this. Should I use my fingers or dick?" My dick was trickling up with blood just thinking about invading his ass.

"Dick please." He grabbed a condom from his wallet and tossed it to me. I rolled it down my hard shaft.

I put his knees over my shoulders and pushed into his hole. I loved watching his wet dick lay against his toned belly. I was slowly sliding in.

"That's it, you can fuck me. I've done this before," Shane said.

I loved to see him completely undone, begging for me. His neat hair completely disheveled.

"Right." I pushed in and slid home. Balls deep.

In and out I slammed into his ass, the sound of our bodies smacking together echoed in his apartment. It was louder than the TV!

I came again, quicker than I thought I could.

"That's it," Shane rasped, "fuck me like you mean it." I attempted to fuck him harder.

"That's a good boy," he rasped. Hearing that completely undid me.

"I'm coming!" I shouted. Shane jerked his dick once, twice and was shooting a load all over his stomach and mine.

I kissed a guy, and I liked it. But the sex was even better.

It probably wasn't polite to kiss and tell, but that's exactly what I was going to do!

So... Maybe I was gay after all.

The End

CHEATING ON MY GIRLFRIEND

Straight to gay erotica

Kyle Rayne

It's inevitable that a guy will break up with his girlfriend at some point in his life. It's been on my mind for a while. This isn't working for me. Her personality is pleasant to be around, and she's a nice lady. What's up with me saying that without enthusiasm? I mean... She wants to fuck all the time! Like most guys, I should be thrilled. I hate it because it's just a chore. There's nothing fun or enjoyable about it.

You shouldn't make fun of me because sometimes I can't finish. When I'm around her, my dick completely deflates. There's such a thing as ED... Except that my dick doesn't malfunction when I masturbate.

This is clearly a sign. This is my body's reaction to break it off. I have no chemistry with her physically or biologically! It's her, not my dick. My plumbing works just fine, thank you very much. When she's not around, I can stroke my dick and ejaculate just fine. This guy doesn't need Viagra...

I didn't tell her I was coming over. Three times I've circled the block of her apartment complex, thinking of what to say.

"It's not you, it's me." I know it's dumb and cliche but it's the truth.

When I knocked on her door, a man said, "Come in!" His voice was familiar; it was her brother's best friend. Sam was shirtless behind the counter when I walked into the apartment!

"You just missed her. She left with her brother."

"When is she going to be back?"

"They left for the weekend. I'm here to watch the cat."

My girlfriend didn't tell me she was leaving for the weekend, so I didn't say anything.

"You look shocked," Sam said.

Nervously, I ran my hands through my hair. "Yeah, well, I wanted to talk to her in person."

My stupid eyes kept scanning down his chest and abs behind the kitchen counter instead of looking at his face. There was something tantalizing about his chest, lightly dusted with dark hair. His hips and legs piqued my interest—I wanted to see them. Weird, huh?

My gaze shifted back to Sam when he snapped his fingers. It was embarrassing to get caught checking him out.

Wait, what am I saying? I was not checking out a man. There is *not* a man on my radar.

Instead of saying, 'eyes up here,' Sam said, "Let me get you a beer."

"Ok, sure."

"We have the place to ourselves this weekend, and I didn't want to drink alone."

I nearly choked on my tongue as he walked over to the refrigerator. Except for a pair of socks, he was naked. Did it seem weird that I wanted him to take off his socks? Yes, it's fucking weird.

He had an ass so hard I could probably bounce a quarter off of it. It wouldn't jiggle if I spanked him.

It's not appropriate to think about spanking another man. Hey, I like spanking and my soon-to-be-ex girlfriend never was into kink-play.

My lips parted in disgust, and I stammered, "Fuck dude! Why are you naked?" My god, he was fit. He looked like a Greek god. My body didn't look like that.

With a deep voice, he said, "I wasn't expecting company." He bent down and rummaged through the bottom shelf. I nearly groaned when I saw his balls poking out from between his thighs. Standing up, he turned around. He held two beers and a bag of chips in one hand.

His junk caught my attention and I couldn't look away. There was definitely a penis there... with big perky balls dusted with hair. He sat the chips and beers on the countertop near me. Opening a drawer, he grabbed a bottle opener.

I stepped back, I yelled, "Get that elephant trunk away from me."

As he cracked open a beer, a wry smile spread across his face. I swear he pushed his hips out to accentuate the size of his package. "Don't be so shy. It's just a penis and balls like yours. Elephant trunk huh? You think I'm big? I didn't peg you as a 'Size-Queen.'"

I stood there frozen. "A Size-Queen?" I've never heard that term before, but I understood it well enough. He had a big fucking dick. "No, you've got it wrong. That's not what I meant."

His lips twitched with a chuckle, "Drink the beer and relax. Let me get a pair of shorts." He turned to walk away, looking back over his shoulder. "Don't run away from me while I'm getting dressed."

Oddly, that thought didn't occur to me. In fact, I wanted to drink a beer with Sam and unwind. It was still weighing on my mind that I hadn't broken up with my girlfriend...

Sipping my beer, I plopped down on the couch. Sam sat down next to me, fully clothed. He wore a gray t-shirt and jeans. As he drank his beer, he smiled.

"She didn't tell you that they were going on a trip?"

He was a preceptive fucker. "Nope."

"Fuck, man. I'm sorry to hear that. Want some tequila?"

As I finished my beer, I said, "No thanks on the tequila. Did they tell you where they were going?"

"No, and I didn't ask." An awkward silence followed. "Did you want to tell her something?"

Taking a deep breath, I exhaled. "I wanted to end our relationship in person. I could do it via text message, except I'm not a dick."

I felt Sam's hand on my shoulder. "In today's world, it wouldn't be considered a big deal. You didn't get any courtesy by knowing where she went."

"My mama raised me better than that. There's no way I'm doing that."

Then Sam tackled me and pulled my phone out of my pocket. "I'll help you with that." My strength was no match for his. I was pinned down on the couch by his big, strong body. In a way, I liked it...

While playing keep away, he opened my text messages.

"Hey, that stuff is private!"

When he began reading my texts, I tried to grab my phone.

"Why do you care so much anyway? This really isn't any of your business."

When he handed me my phone back, he said, "I wrote the message for you. I won't send the text, but you will. I know someone that is interested in you, so it is my business."

"Really?"

He looked deeply into my eyes as he leaned forward. "Yes, that's true. This person would treat you better. There is no way they would leave on a weekend trip without you. Often they work during the day, so you would sleep with them with them at night."

My Adam's apple bobbled in my throat as I gulped. All I could say was, "Really? Who's interested in me?"

Sam touched my thigh with his hand. "It's me, of course." My heart raced at what he implied.

"Sam, I've never..."

"You have never been with a man, I know."

He leant forward and kissed my neck lightly. His lips touched the back of my neck as he kissed it. "Does that feel good?"

My spine tingled with the sensations. "Yes."

The way he caressed my hair and wrapped his arms around my neck felt wonderful. I leaned forward and moaned as he kissed my neck and fuck... I loved when he sucked my earlobe into his mouth. Why did that feel so good? His mouth was so wet and warm.

"You like that huh?" he rasped.

"It's just... Women really don't kiss men like that."

I felt his fingers running sensuously through my hair and his lips kissing the underside of my chin. I felt sensations all over my body.

"My ex never tried to make me feel good. It was all one-sided."

"Let me show you how good I can make you feel," he purred.

"Ok."

"Good."

His raspy voice sent shivers down my spine, all the way to my dick. Blood was pumping through my cock. My wood was definitely sprouting.

"Okay, but what about my girlfriend who isn't my ex...yet?"

In spite of the fact that I was over the relationship, it felt wrong to cheat. My relationship with her ended months ago.

With a pec, he kissed my lips. My freshly shaven face felt great against his casual scruff. With his hands, he continued mapping my body and sensually kissing me.

"I'll let you decide. I won't stop you from leaving now. Or..."

"Or what?" I asked with curiosity.

I melted when he licked my lips across the seam. The feeling was amazing. I was fucked when he licked my lips again.

"Let's have sex now, and you can text her when we're done. We don't have to bother her when we're busy. Isn't that right?" He licked my lips again. "She was too busy for you. She's probably done with you too, but didn't tell you."

She might not technically be my burden of a girlfriend. Perfect!

I wrapped my arms around his neck.

I rasped, "Ok, let's do this. Be patient with me. I don't know what I'm supposed to do."

I had a very hard dick—unlike with my ex.

My body didn't want her—but it wants him.

My dick is so hard that it's throbbing against my pants—I want him!

"I'll take it slow and we'll do whatever feels right. There's no need to try everything tonight," he rasped.

As he peeled off his shirt, his glorious body was revealed.

"Throughout the months, we'll explore your sexuality at your own pace."

Oh fuck, he did want me. Usually, no one wants me. No one is patient with me.

As he kissed me passionately, I could feel the heat flushing my dick. He flicked his tongue around in my mouth. My tongue slid into his mouth as I reciprocated his kiss. His scruff, smell, and taste were all very masculine—I loved it.

He teased my trail of hair under my navel with his calloused fingers. He slowly explored my body, working his way up to my pecs. I moaned as he thumbed my nipples. They had never been played with before.

Sam broke off our kiss and said, "You can touch me if you want, but don't feel obligated."

"Okay," I replied shyly.

Using my fingertips, I traced down his chest and abs. The curves and valleys of his abs captivated me. My fingers caressed his strong arms before falling on his lap.

"Can you take your pants off again?"

"Of course." As he stood up, he began tearing at his belt, button, and zipper.

"And your boxers and socks," I added.

"Whatever you want." I've never seen anyone strip so quickly.

"Feel free to touch my body and examine it until you're comfortable getting naked with me."

"Okay."

That was an offer I couldn't refuse. My hands traced patterns in his hair as I explored his chest. It wasn't enough for me. I wanted more.

"I'll get naked."

Even though I was feeling shy, my boner was stuck at an odd angle in my boxers. As I undressed, Sam watched me with rapt attention.

Sam was naked on the couch, his thighs were spread wide open. For some reason, the crack of his ass under his balls was the sexiest thing I've ever seen. It was the first time I had seen a naked man other than myself.

My hands rested on his knees as I stood between his legs. His dick was jutting straight up in the air. His dick was thick and veiny... so sexy.

"Should we keep kissing?" Sam asked.

I dropped to my knees. "No. I mean yes. I want to kiss your cock."

"You don't have to."

"I want to taste you."

I received a curt nod as consent. His dick head glistened with wet, clear pre-cum. I wiped my finger across his tip to get the juices. Before I put his dick in my mouth, I tasted him with my finger.

"Fuck," I rasped. "You taste amazing."

"Is that right? It tastes better fresh off the tap," he teasingly said.

His dick looked delicious! To tease me, he held his dick and tapped it on his stomach—he was hard. I knelt down and placed my hands on his thighs. I wanted his legs to be as wide as possible... and I sucked his cock right into my mouth.

"Fuck," he moaned.

I never liked eating pussy but I loved sucking dick. It would become addictive to me. My head bobbed up and down as I sucked his length. Even though Sam's body was still, he was moaning like crazy. He wasn't thrusting his hips because he didn't want to gag me. I spit his dick out.

"Don't be afraid to thrust your hips up. Don't treat me like a rookie."

"Have it your way." He rubbed his fingers through my hair, grabbed my skull, and pushed his dick back into my mouth.

"That's it, you suck dick so good."

I loved watching him flex his hips up when he pushed into my mouth. I loved how he face-fucked me. But I wanted to taste something else. I just lifted my head and didn't say anything. I cupped his sac and licked his taint, and licked down his crack. He moaned so intensely it was like a growl.

"F-fuck, that feels good." I pressed my tongue into his crack. He tasted faintly of soap. Those sexy-smelling soaps for men.

"You just took a shower?" I teased.

"I just stepped out of the shower when you knocked on the door."

I slung his legs over my shoulders. I spread his ass cheeks wide with my hands. I found what I was looking for. His pink, fleshy and quivering hole.

My tongue circled around it, but it wasn't enough. My tongue licked across it, loving how tight it felt against my tongue. I licked him all over, from his balls to his taint and his hole.

"Let's go to bed, I wanna suck your dick too," Sam said.

"Okay, sounds good."

I was going to fuck a man in my ex's bed. Hooray for me! There was no way we were going to bone in her brother's bed.

"On your back," he ordered. My cock jutted up in the air as I lay flat. He climbed on top of me and sank his dick into my mouth. It makes sense now what he wanted to do—Sixty nine.

I gave him a good hard smack on the ass. I could tell he liked it by his giggle. He had a perfect ass for spanking. I could spank his ass all day. But first, sucking dick...

The two of us were sucking each other's dicks. It's the hottest thing I've ever done! The ass of this man was right in front of my face, right where I wanted it to be. Using my finger, I wiped some spit off his wet shaft. My finger was sticky and wet, so I stuck it in his ass. As he moaned onto my shaft, I knew he wanted me to keep pushing. It's my first time, but I wanted to try it. My almost-ex-girlfriend always shot me down when I wanted to try anal. She was no fun.

My finger slid in and out of Sam's ass and I was fascinated by his reactions. I noticed how his hole trembled around my finger. His thighs trembled as he moaned. His sac was high and tight. As soon as he orgasmed, I was going to swallow him down. I would drink every last drop out of his balls.

With the help of his tongue, Sam worked up and down my shaft with his hand. I didn't know how long I would last. It was so hot to have sex with another man. I was going to blow my load into his mouth.

I felt him press a finger into my crack and circle my hole, but he never touched it. By circling it, he teased me. The sensation there hadn't occurred to me before. My sensitive flesh felt amazing under the pressure of his touch. I wanted more... so much more. I was about to cum and I wanted it to be as intense as possible. I grabbed his wrist and pressed a finger at my hole.

"Stick a finger in me, please," I rasped like a needy bitch.

The only response I got from him was to moan on my shaft as he kept sucking my length. His finger pushed deep into my taboo void. He was deep... so deep... fucking me with a thick, calloused finger.

The next time we had sex, I wanted his dick inside me. Even fantasizing about it made my nuts tingle. The pleasure burned through my groin, especially when Sam slurped on my dick. Those sloppy, wet sounds were so hot. As well as flicking his tongue on my crown every time his mouth got to my head.

I spit his dick out. "Oh fuck Sam, I'm coming so fucking hard!"

I pumped my load deep into his throat. Sam's dick wasn't forgotten, though. I jerked it in a crisscross pattern. That's how I like to stroke my dick.

His dick started shooting out all over my stomach. I've never seen anything more sexy. With his juices, my new boyfriend completely saturated my stomach and chest. As he gulped my load down the back of his throat.

Despite my dick going soft and my balls being drained, he kept sucking it. It was getting so sensitive for me. My flaccid dick was still in his mouth when I pulled it out.

"That's enough for today!"

"Can I see you tomorrow?" He asked so sweetly and shyly.

"C'mere." I pulled him into my arms. "Of course. We'll do this for as long as you want."

Over the weekend, everything seemed to fly by. Because of my ex's cat, we spent the night. It all worked out in the end. At least I called instead of texting her. She was out of town with her brother and new boyfriend! And she forgot to tell me about it!

We were in my apartment finally. "There's something I want to try." I nudged Sam with my foot while lying in bed naked.

"Oh? What's that?"

I was still shy because we were just getting to know each other.

I whispered in his ear, "Will you fuck me in the ass, please?"

Sam caressed my ass cheeks. "Of course. I'll make you feel so good, I promise."

"Will it hurt?"

"It will sting only for a second, but after that, it will be pleasure you never experienced before."

I trusted him. Besides, I played with myself in the shower a couple days ago. It felt good and I wanted more...

I got on all fours and put my ass in the air, exposing myself to him. He was the only person who ever saw me this way.

"If it hurts, we can stop. I don't need this to feel satisfied."

"I want it." I wanted it to bad that I felt like a needy bitch.

I felt Sam lick my hole and moisten it with his spit. His tongue flicked across my flesh and fuck... it felt good. I couldn't wait to feel him bury his dick inside of me.

"I'll lube my cock," Sam explained.

I felt his thick head press into my opening—my untouched place. The place I wanted to wreck...

"Oh G-god," I moaned. I was burning with pleasurable sensations. MY whole body erupted as he sank his dick deeper... and deeper... until he was balls deep.

"Fuck me," I begged with my face buried in pillows. "I want it hard and deep."

"Of course babe, anything you want."

He fucked me deep, hard and slow. With every thrust of his cock, I felt my orgasm building.

There was something magical about hearing his moans and feeling our bodies smack against one another. The wet sounds made by his dick sliding into and out of my ass was a treat for my ears.

As I reached between my legs, I lazily jerked my dick back and forth. Getting fucked in the ass was enough to push me over the edge. I blew my load on my bedsheets. My bed was soaked with ropes of hot, wet and sticky cum. I wondered who would sleep in the wet spot...

"Oh F-fuck!" Sam screamed. "I'm coming so hard!"

Then I felt Sam pumping his load deep into my ass. That was a fucking amazing feeling.

The end

TOUCH ME

Straight to gay erotica

Kyle Rayne

I keep getting funny looks from my coworker Danny. Funny in a different way than 'ha-ha' funny. It's difficult to explain... he just stares at me weirdly. Maybe it's because I'm the new guy at work. Nothing compares to being a new lawyer at a firm. It's like being thrown into a shark tank. This job was hard earned, so I won't let a grumpy jerk ruin it.

I came to the office on a Saturday. Normally, I wouldn't be here, but a friend asked me to take on a pro bono case. I couldn't work on the case when I was on the clock, so I stopped by the office. My cubicle isn't empty, there's someone else here...

"What are you doing here Danny?" I asked while sipping my coffee.

"I could ask you the same thing," he said with a condescending tone.

"Now that we're off the clock," I calmly replied, "you shouldn't be a dick to me just because I'm new."

There was a five-o'clock shadow on his chin, and his square-shaped jaw hung open. That's when I noticed he was barefoot. He wore slacks and a button-down shirt that was neatly tucked in.

"Where are your shoes and socks?" I asked, shocked.

He had very naked feet. I wasn't the type of guy who has a kink for feet. The sight of naked and exposed feet played tricks on my mind. It made me wonder what his other body parts would look like naked...

Taking a sip of his own coffee before speaking, he looked down at his naked feet. "I didn't know anyone would be here. For the record, I'm not a dick just because you're new."

"Okay, fair enough. Are you gonna tell me why? I need to know if we're going to work together."

He sat his coffee down on my desk. Our chests were almost touching as he stepped closer to me. Because I was curious about what he would do, I didn't want to step away.

"We're off the clock, so sexual harassment complaints to HR don't count. You know that right?"

I was caught off guard by his comment. My Adam's apple bobbed in my throat as I swallowed. "You're right, I guess."

Taking a step closer, he backed me up to my desk. As I sat on top of it, he caged me in with his legs.

"What the fuck Danny?"

He cupped my chin and caressed it with his thumb. He rasped, "You're beautiful." His dark gaze smoldered right into my eyes. Suddenly, I realized everything—it all made sense. My breath hitched in my throat. My palms were sweating.

"That's what this is about? You're attracted... to *me*?"

He grabbed the desk behind him and dropped my chin. His lips were so close to mine I could kiss him. Except I'm a straight man, so I wouldn't do that...

"Yes, I'm attracted to you. But you're about to tell me that you're a straight man. Isn't that right?"

I was caged by his big body, pinned to the desk. There's just one problem... I don't want him to move. It feels like I want him close to me... touching me.

Looking for an answer, he scans my eyes.

"I... I don't know." My mind is racing in a different direction right now. More specifically, in a non-linear and not straight way. I find myself... wanting to kiss him.

"It's okay if you don't know. Maybe I should move?" Danny asks.

There was no doubt in my mind that I felt... curious.

"No, stay here," I said. His face was shocked, but he didn't move a muscle.

As he places his hands on my shoulders, he clears his throat. "Let's go on a date. Afterwards, if you decide that you don't want to date a man, no hard feelings."

I feel my heart pounding in my chest. Blood is flowing south to my dick because my heart is beating so hard and so fast. Feeling my cock pump up makes me want to try new things...

Wrapping my arms around his neck, I embrace him.

"We'll go on a date." I felt brave and kissed him on the cheek. "But I want you to kiss me first."

"Okay, of course," Danny rasped with deep, husky voice. "I'll kiss you."

He tugged at the tie around his neck to loosen it. I didn't want to ask why he wore it. Suddenly, I was glad he had it on. I imagined tying him to his desk with it...

He gripped the nape of my neck and continued, "Only if you're sure." I didn't say anything. The only thing left for me to do

80

was to act...

As I leaned forward, I pressed my lips against his—I kissed him.

There was something different about a man's mouth. It just felt different in a good way. His scruff tickled my freshly shaven face and fuck... It made my dick harder. His touch, his taste, his smell... It was all very masculine and very sexy...

There was something sexy and masculine about everything he did... The way he was touching me and moaning.

My tongue slid into his mouth as I pressed my lips against his—I groaned. We were both hard.

His tongue and taste tantalized me in ways I didn't know existed. Our tongues swirled together as we kissed. Danny flicked his tongue everywhere, exploring every centimeter of my mouth. I moaned and pressed my hips against him. I could feel his rod through his pants. His dick was hard, like mine. My instinct was to dry hump him.

Danny was such a good kisser. He kissed passionately and intensely. I could make out with him for hours in my bed. Or on my desk. Or on the carpeted office floor.

As we kissed, I grabbed Danny's tie and dropped to my knees, taking him with me. I kept my grip on his tie as he moaned into my mouth. As much as I wanted to be on top of him, I wasn't sure if it was too soon. I was going to test him and see if he would let me push him down and mount him.

With one hand wrapped around his tie, I gripped the nape of his neck with the other. I gently pushed him back and lay down on top of him.

A wry smile spread across his face and he huffed in amusement.

"You're enthusiastic... for a straight man," he goaded me, "Your dick seems to think you aren't straight."

Dammit, he was right. My dick was so hard that it was painful.

"I haven't been laid in a while," was my excuse.

Danny's eyes lit up with excitement. He teasingly said, "So, tell me, are you going to get laid tonight?"

I pushed my hips into his, making our dicks grind together. "Not tonight, but hopefully now."

"Oh?" he coyly said like a tease. "We're going to have a tryst in the office?" I rubbed his dick over his pants, and fuck, his girth was thick. "Should we go back to my apartment?" Danny added.

"No, we're doing this right here, right now." I sounded like a sex-starved maniac. It's okay though... because I was.

As I kissed Danny again, I ran my fingers through his short hair. Even though it wasn't long enough to grab, I liked the way it felt between my fingers. I knew what else I would like between my fingers...

I frantically undid his belt buckle, button, and zipper. He kicked his legs to shimmy his pants off. Taking a look down, he was a whitey-tighty guy. I don't know why it turned me on more for some reason. He was also frantically removing my pants. Neither of us had taken off our shirts.

"Let's take our shirts off. We both look like Tom Cruise in that famous movie scene."

"Agreed."

A blink of an eye later, we were both sprawled out naked on the carpet of the office. We were a tangle of limbs and sloppy, aggressive kisses. These were the bruising-type kisses—that type of kissing always made my dick the hardest.

I was on top of Danny and I shoved my dick into his stomach. Then our cocks were grinding together. His dick was so thick... The tip was flushed red with blood.

His naked body was so sexy. He was very much in shape, but not bloated from creatine. Danny was hardly a beefcake. His body was slender, yet lean with natural muscles. I'd never seen anything so sexy. The thin hair that dusted his chest and the hair under his navel that trailed to the base of his dick were particularly sexy to me. I hadn't touched his cock yet... I'd never touched a cock except for mine. I wanted to do it.

We were fooling around on the office floor, which was grossly inappropriate, but ask me if I care...

I sucked Danny's bottom lip into my mouth, released it, then asked, "Can I touch your dick?"

He cracked a smile. "You are such a polite lover. Yes, of course you can touch my dick." He grabbed me and rolled me on my side. "This is more comfortable, so we can stroke each other."

"Fuck, alright." We used our clothes as pillows. I was using Danny's slacks and shirt. I buried my face in his clothes and inhaled his scent before I licked my hand, and wrapped it around his dick. I glided my hand up and down his shaft.

"F-fuck, oh, fuck," Danny groaned and writhed under my touch.

My hand got dry, so I licked it again and fisted his cock. My mind was just registering that Danny was stroking me with his eyes scrunched and lidded heavily with lust.

Another man was jerking me off and I fucking loved it. How did I now know this about myself until now?

It was mind-blowing how Danny stroked me up and down. In order to hold my skin in place, he held the base of my dick. As his hand slid up and down, I felt more friction. The only person who could stroke another man's dick like that would be a man.

Never before had I seen anything so sexy... my dick's crown appearing and disappearing from his fist. I was leaking so much precum, it was dripping down. My shaft was wet from so much moisture.

Already my nuts were tingling... I didn't think I'd last much longer. As we jerked each other off, we were lying naked on our sides. It was so fucking hot.

Then Danny grabbed my hand and pressed it into the crack of his ass.

"Touch me, back here, please," he begged, "Please. It's so hard to jerk my dick and masturbate my ass at the same time."

My dick only hardened when he asked me. "Yeah, of course."

My finger was tickled by hair as I pressed it into his warm crack. After finding his hole, I circled it.

"Oh my God. That ass," I choked out. "I want that ass."

"Then touch me, please."

His hole was there for me to touch. Danny wanted it. My ex-girlfriend was a prude and never let me play with her back door. It was taboo, according to her. That's a straight woman's logic for you. As for me, it was another way to experience pleasure. It was a sexual exploration of the human body.

"I'm going to touch you now."

"Please."

It dawned on me that I needed lubrication. After pulling my finger out of his crack, I stuck it in his mouth. "Wet it for me." He sucked my finger as though he were sucking my cock. Maybe next time he'll suck my dick, but for now...

"Hands and knees for me, baby," I commanded.

"Yes, of course."

Danny got down on all fours. He had his cheek pressed into the carpet, and his sexy ass was raised for me to admire. It was my first time seeing a man like this, and I wanted to enjoy it… savor it as much as I could. Every inch of his body was exposed to me, and I wanted to see it all. Reaching between his legs, I cupped his heavy sac. His nuts were full and tight. I could tell he needed to cum. He probably jacked off a few days ago, judging from what I could tell.

"You need to come, baby?"

"Yes, I do."

"I'll make you cum. I'm going to make you feel so good," I rasped. I wanted to taste him. Sitting on the carpet with my legs crossed, I leaned forward and licked his hole.

"Holy shit!" he cried out, "F-fuck!"

Fuck, I didn't know Danny very well, and I might have crossed a line. Suddenly, I felt like a dick and pulled away, even though I didn't want to. I liked the way his tight ring of muscle felt against my tongue.

"Should I stop?"

Over his shoulder, he glanced back at me. "No, it felt really good. It's just… No one has ever done that to me before."

It's not my place to pry into his business, but his ex's were probably prudes, too. I never claimed to be an entirely straightlaced person… I liked to explore my sexuality and didn't think I was doing anything wrong.

As I gripped his ass cheeks, I spread them wide. Through the muscle barrier, I pressed my tongue into his ass.

"Oh my fucking God... that feels so good," Danny moaned and that gave me an idea.

By pulling out my tongue, I replaced it with my pointer finger. As I slid my finger in and out of his ass, I flicked my tongue around his hole.

I loved watching his pink flesh wrap around my finger. It didn't take me long to figure out what else I wanted that flesh wrapped around.

My dick needed to be swallowed by his cute lil' ass. Since I didn't know him that well, I wasn't sure how to ask. I pulled my tongue and finger away.

"Danny, I was wondering... Do you...?" Oh fuck, I got shy and backed out at the last minute.

Danny's face was flushed pink, along with his dick.

"I have a condom in my wallet, if that's what you're asking," Danny replied.

I was such a stupid ass. Of course I forgot about the condom... Maybe after Danny and I got to know each other better, I could bareback him. I wanted to feel him from the inside, skin to skin. But not today...

"Yes, that's exactly what I was asking for. Can you get it for me?" I handed Danny his pants. He frantically pulled a condom out of his wallet and handed it to me.

"You'll really like these condoms. They are super-wet with lube."

"That is the best invention ever," I said while rolling the condom down my shaft. It was wet, sticky and perfect for what we were about to do.

"Lay down on your back," Danny said and playfully shoved my chest.

"Yes sir," I huffed out a chuckle.

"Whatever, just hold still until I'm all the way in," Danny said. I appreciated him guiding me because I literally knew nothing about how not to hurt someone during anal sex.

Danny straddled my hips and put his ass right on my cock. He held the base and started to slide down my rain-coated shaft.

"You prepped me really good, so I can go kinda quick this time."

"Right." Again, I felt like an inexperienced dumbass, but I was suddenly determined to learn to be a considerate lover. I hoped that's what Danny would be when we were done... I didn't want this to be a one-time thing.

I could feel the warmth of his ass through the rubber and fuck... He was warm and tight... so tight.

"Oh my fucking God," I moaned, "You are so tight."

His ass was better than any pussy I've ever had. This made me realize I could never go back to that. In a vivid realization, I couldn't believe that I ever thought I was straight. A straight man wouldn't be fucking his co-workers' brains out on the office rug.

I watched my dick disappear into his ass. He was now fully seated, my dick completely buried inside of him.

He placed his hands on my chest. "I'm ready, you can fuck me now."

"Aright, of course."

A part of me couldn't believe this was happening. My brain almost couldn't register the fact that I was fucking another man. I thrust my hips up and down, my ass pressed into the carpet. I grasped Danny's hips for better leverage and I fucked him deep, hard and slow. I wasn't in any hurry to cum.

I loved watching my dick glide in and out of his ass. And I loved watching Danny lazily stroke his cock while I fucked him.

But fuck, I was going to cum quickly. His ass was so tight and the sensation of it quivering around my shaft was so new to me. His cute little ass was milking my dick, squeezing it and releasing it.

"Oh fuck Danny," I moaned, "I'm going to cum soon."

"I want to cum too."

He fisted his cock and stroked it while I fucked him. Oh my God, I'd never seen anything so sexy. His fist wrapped around his dick while I fucked his ass. My nuts were hugged up tight to my body and I was going to cum.

I reached up and firmly gripped the nape of his neck and pulled him down so I could kiss him. He moaned and almost shrieked into my mouth. I hadn't realized that changing the angle of my dick might hurt him.

"Are you ok?"

"I'm more than ok! Your dick is so deep. It feels so good, it surprised me!"

Our mouths were a tangle of tongues. My dick was deep in his ass and it was tight... so tight and wet from my spit and the lube. Sensations shot up from my balls, through my dick and my load pumped into the condom. It was like my body was shattering with each pump of cum that drained from my dick. I've never cum so hard.

"I'm coming!" I shouted.

"Me too," Danny rasped and he jerked his dick once... twice and he was blowing his load all over my chest. Thick, white cream was shooting out of his slit. I didn't hesitate to wipe a finger through it and taste his juices. Well damn, I was surprised that I actually liked the taste.

Danny collapsed on top of me. Our chests were sticky with the cooling jiz. I could get used to this... We kept kissing for what felt like forever. I suddenly felt like a teenager all over again.

I stopped when I heard my stomach grumble. After all that fucking, I was starving!

"Let's get dressed," I told Danny.

We both walked to the office bathroom naked. I used some paper towels to clean off my chest. The cleaning job wasn't perfect, but as matter of fact, I liked a little bit of his cum stuck in my chest hair. When we went out to dinner, it would be our dirty little secret. It was as if I had an animalistic instinct that wanted me to be soaked in his jiz.

We cleaned up and got dressed. Both of our previously neatly ironed clothes were rumpled and wrinkly. It was perfect! We looked like a pair of fucked-out messes. Danny attempted to flatten his hair with his hands and smooth out the creases on his shirt. He has been utterly quiet since we stopped kissing.

"No, no Danny." I pulled him in for a hug. "Don't make this awkward. I'm taking you out to a dinner-date just like that."

"I look like a mess."

"You're a fucked-out mess. That's the perfect look for you."

And when we were finished with our dinner, I paid. "Come spend the night at my place," I told Danny. I specifically didn't ask him. I told him what I wanted. I wanted... needed to take him to my bed. I wanted to drench my sheets in our cum. I wanted my pillows to smell like him.

His cheeks flushed red, "Sure, Okay. I'll spend the night."

"You can borrow some clean clothes from me."

The sight of his naked body sprawled out in my bed was one of the sexiest things I had ever seen in my life. There was no doubt in my mind that I would fuck him into the mattress. The only thing I wanted to do to him was wreck him. It was my goal to make him cum so hard that he would scream my name as loud as he could and forget about everything else in the world.

The End

EXPERIMENTING WITH MY BEST FRIEND

Straight to gay erotica

Kyle Rayne

I was watching Netflix with my best friend and we were just chilling out. When I said we were 'chilling,' we were actually lying in my bed. It's nothing new, we've been doing it since we were kids. I can justify it for two reasons.

Number one: the bigger TV is in my bedroom.

Number two: My bed is more comfortable than the couch.

My best friend Alex—the two of us were so comfortable together. I saw him come into my room with a bowl of popcorn and take off his jeans and lay on top of my comforter. We've been doing this for years.

As I scrolled through endless movies, I couldn't decide what to watch. Alex had already started eating the popcorn. As I glanced down, I noticed the button on his boxers was undone.

My eyes were glued to the opening when I said, "Your fly is open." A crease of skin was visible to my naked eye, and fuck, I almost groaned. *What was wrong with me?*

"It's not technically my fly, but whatever."

My mind suddenly wandered to what his dick looked like as he fastened the button. It wasn't the first time I had thought about it. As much as I hate to admit it, I occasionally jerk my dick while fantasizing about it in the shower.

"What do you want to watch tonight?" Alex asked.

The only thing I could think of to say was, "Porn."

He stared at me wide-eyed. "Dude, we haven't done that since high school." He didn't mention it, but we used to jerk off in my bed while lying next to one another. Yeah, I was implying exactly that.

As soon as I clicked my TV over to the browser, I typed in my favorite porn site.

"Come on dude, not tonight." Alex grabbed the remote from me. Somehow, the remote clicked on my 'favorite-list' when he grabbed it.

"Gay porn?" he asked, shocked.

Now was the perfect time to air my dirty laundry.

"Don't judge me, it's hot."

With a deep, hard stare, he looked into my eyes. I felt like he was searching my soul for answers.

"Is there anything you would like to tell me?" he asked.

I grabbed the bowl of popcorn and set it down on my nightstand. I put my hand on his shoulder to see if he would pull back.

"Alex, I've wanted you for a long time."

He flicked my hand off his shoulder, stood up, and put on his jeans again. It hurt to be rejected, and he was silent. When he stomped out of my room, I yelled, "It's not worth losing our friendship over!"

Fuck, I knew this would happen. That's why I never made a move on him before.

Guess I'm gonna spend another lonely night watching porn and stroking my dick. Scrolling down, I found my favorite video. I've jerked my dick countless times while watching this video.

There's something so sensual about the way the guys kiss slowly and explore each other's bodies.

Kissing... Touching...

I am blown away by their onscreen chemistry. In one kiss, he begins at the stomach and works his way up to the chest. He kisses his way back down. There's a part where he kisses his dick over his boxers and fuck, and I can't get enough of it.

My dick was swollen with blood, so I removed my briefs and reached for lube in my nightstand. I squirted an ample amount of lube in my palm and smoothed it over my shaft. My cock was itching to be jerked slowly by my hand. In my mind, I didn't want to come so quickly because it would mean my night was basically over. Suddenly, Alex burst into my room as I stroked my dick.

"Can we talk?" He covered his eyes when he saw me stroking my dick. "Geezus dude, I've been outta your room for five minutes."

He breathed heavily as his eyes locked on the porn. In this part, the power-bottom gets sucked before he gets fucked. Alex was frozen in place.

"I told you it was hot."

I didn't stop masturbating... In front of my best friend. Alex glanced away from the TV and gazed at my hand stroking my cock.

"You can watch me instead of the porn," I teased. I reached for my remote.

"Leave it on," he said.

Then I threw him my lube at him and rasped deeply, "Don't be a bitch and take your pants off." Then I added, "And your boxers."

I didn't think he would do it, but he did. Like countless times before, I watched him take off his pants. But this time was different. This time, it was sexual, and nothing got me more excited. For the first time, he slid his boxers down and exposed his junk. He was sporting a semi. Damn, he had a thick girth! Even though I had more length, I wasn't thick *like that.* My mouth was watering at the thought of seeing his dick fully erect.

Like he's done for years, he lay down next to me. Except this time, he's naked. Although I wanted to touch him, I knew I had to be patient. He might run away from me if I push him too hard. I groaned as he stroked his nice thick cock.

"Fuck, you're sexier than the guys in the porn," I rasped.

He kept stroking his dick as he huffed in amusement. His eyes were glued to my TV with rapt attention.

"I knew you'd like this one, it's my favorite too," I said.

He glared at me with a 'fuck-off' look. While watching my friend stroke his dick, I lazily stroked mine. His thigh twitched when I put my other hand on it.

I kept my hand there to test him. "Don't be so skittish," I said and stroked his thigh. "We've known each other for years, this shouldn't be awkward."

"Whatever dude."

"I want to touch you. Let me stroke your dick."

"That's so gay," he whispered.

We were touching thighs as I scooted close to him.

"If you touch your cock, does it count as gay?" I knew my logic was contorted, but it was worth a shot.

"No," he chuckled.

"Then what makes it gay if I touch yours?"

He didn't respond. My hands caressed his hips and I stopped right next to his dick.

"I love touching my dick and making it feel good. I can do the same for you. It's not *gay*," I assured him.

A wry smile spread across his face. "You're insane," he remarked. "It's totally gay to touch another man's dick."

Feeling brave, I kissed his neck. "I know it's gay, but I was just fucking with you. Now ask me if I care." I kept kissing his neck. Fuck, I loved the scent of his scruff and the way it felt against my lips.

"Are you gay?" There was a rasp to his voice, like he had been eating gravel.

"Yes, I'm gay. Can we have sex now?"

I was kissing his cheek and working my way to his lips. When I reached his lips, I bit his bottom lip and he groaned.

"Okay, you win." He threw himself at me and wrapped his arms around my neck, kissing me passionately. It's always been on my bucket list to kiss a guy—I've never done it before. I'm glad I waited for my best friend. It was everything I'd dreamed of and more.

I felt my bottom lip get sucked up into his warm, wet mouth. Instead, I imagined that my tongue was my dick. I'd eventually get my dick in his mouth. My heart pounded when I tasted blood after he bit it. With bruising-type kisses, he fiercely kissed me—I groaned.

He kissed me ravenously and passionately. As I moaned into his mouth, I said, "Oh f-fuck Alex. You've got some pent-up sexual energy."

To my surprise, he grabbed my shoulders and pushed me into the mattress. His hands were on my chest and his breath was heaving like he'd just run a mile.

"If we do this, what does it say about me?" he asked. With his question, I treaded cautiously.

"That you're bisexual?" I said it like a question because I was questioning him. I wasn't going to accuse him of being gay.

Our chests were pressed together as he lowered himself over me. His hips were at my side, and I wanted to press his balls against mine, but it could wait.

I watched him gaze into my eyes. "I've got a problem. Actually, I'm not a fan of pussy."

"Me neither and there's nothing wrong with that."

As he lightly touched my chest, fingering my body hair, he groaned, "I don't like tits."

"Me neither. I never have." I kissed him before he could start talking again. Kissing him shut him up fast.

I wanted to make him cum so hard he would scream my name and see stars. My next wish was for him to sleep in my bed tonight. But first, it was time for my best friend to experience everything I could offer. I'd give him pleasure and more. I was determined to give him everything he wanted. Maybe he'll realize he's gay later.

Now our dicks were sandwiched between our stomachs, pressed together by his body. The moisture of his cum on my skin made me want to taste him—fuck.

I broke our kiss. "I wanna suck your dick. Let me lick all the sweet precum off of you."

"Fuck, alright."

He flopped on his back unceremoniously. My bed looked gorgeous with him naked on it, especially with his rumpled hair. It was beautiful to see him naked.

My heart raced—I couldn't wait to see what his cum-face looked like. Also, I couldn't wait to turn him into a boneless fucked-out mess.

I licked his leaking slit, pushing the tip of my tongue into it. The taste of him was delicious—I loved it. There was a sweet saltiness to his flavor. His taste would become addictive to me.

Alex bucked his hips. "H-holy shit dude, I never knew it was so sensitive there."

"I like playing with my slit sometimes."

I was going to do something else he'd probably like. On the underside of his dickhead's V, where the crown is, I flicked my tongue.

He rasped, "F-fuck, that feels good. How do you know to do all this shit?"

"I probably masturbate more than the average American."

I had no shame in my masturbation game. Alex would change that for me anyway... now that he's in my bed. It reminded me how hard it is to finger your own ass and jack off at the same time. A toy would make it easier, but I didn't have one. Now that I've got Alex, I don't need one anyway

After we finished the kissing-foreplay, I sucked his big juicy head into my mouth. I've wanted this for so long, I didn't want him to cum too soon. I wanted him to moan and pull my hair all night long...

"Oh baby," he rasped.

He grabbed my hair in fistfuls and shoved his hips forward. I loved the way his head bounced off the back of my throat! I wanted to do so many things to him, but sucking his dick was at the top of the list.

As I sucked him, I stroked his girth with my hand. The shaft of his dick was corded with veins. There was no doubt that he had a gorgeous cock. In my other hand, I cupped his heavy sac.

His nuts were hugged up high and tight to his body and flushed red. I knew he was going to orgasm soon. I slowed down my sucking pace.

I loved watching his reactions to me pleasuring him. His eyes were tightly shut and scrunched. His cheeks were flushed red. I loved the way his hips moved and how his abs flexed. It was sexy how he drew up his knees and planted his feet firmly on the mattress. The reactions he gave me were all sexy... But I wanted to know if his hole puckered for me. My finger slid under his balls and down his taint.

"Oh fuck! That feels good when you touch me there," he moaned. It was easy to guess he never touched himself there, so I let out a sultry chuckle.

I slid my finger between his warm crack, and some short hair tickled my finger... I like body hair. My finger found what it was looking for, so I circled it.

I looked into his eyes. As his face scrunched with pleasure, he didn't protest, so I pushed my finger into his hole. I wasn't sure if he would enjoy ass-play. From what I could tell about Alex, he was willing to explore his sexuality. After pushing a fingertip into him, I pulled it back out again.

"Please don't stop, I want this," he said in a deep, gruff voice.

A chuckle escaped my lips, "I need to lubricate my finger. I don't want to hurt you."

"Oh," he shyly moaned. "Do you have experience doing this?"

A hint of jealousy lingered in his eyes. My sweet best friend. "Only with myself. I've never done it to anyone else." As I prepped my finger, I kissed him on the ass cheek. "I've waited a long time for you."

"You should have told me before..."

"That's a conversation for another time." It was a good feeling to push my lubed pointer finger into his ass and he moaned in response.

At least I remembered to clip my nails and file the edges. I was prepared, although I've been doing that for a while for Alex, just in case and today it paid off.

As I fingered his ass, I sucked his dick back into my mouth. I didn't want to hurt him by fingering him hard. I just wanted to start prepping him for someday... That special someday when he'd let me top him. I've always fantasized about putting his knees over the crooks of my elbows when I made love to his ass. Sure, doggy-style would be fine. But I wanted to watch him shoot his load all over his stomach. Maybe I'd lick it off him afterward... Someday.

But for now, I gently fingered his ass. I was surprised when he grabbed my wrist and said, "Another finger." Well damn, luckily I clipped all my fingernails. Sometimes I'm lazy and just clip the one finger I fantasized about fingering him with.

I pushed another finger into his ass. He was so fucking tight. So tight and warm and wet with lube. He pushed my head off his cock.

"Wait, I don't want to cum in your mouth," he rasped.

"Oh? Where would you like to cum?" He looked at me shyly, scared to ask what he wanted.

"Alex, we've known each other since we were kids. You don't need to be shy with me. I'm not a random fuck that you dragged home from a bar. You can trust me."

He sat up and whispered in my ear. "Can you fuck me in the ass?"

Oh God, I'm a lucky, lucky man. "Of course babe. Whatever you want." I was going to worship that ass. "I'll make you feel so good."

Like in my favorite fantasy, I spread his legs obscenely wide. All of him was on display for me... and me alone. I'd never let another man see him like this.

I climbed between his legs and put his knees on my elbows. Yep, I knew his feet would look good in the air. His dick was still standing erect and I could see his shaft glistening with precum. I hoped what I was about to do would blow his mind.

I grabbed my dick at the base and slid my head into his warm crack. Oh fuck, he was warm and wet. I pushed my head at the tight ring of muscle and pushed in and Alex jumped.

"Should I stop?"

"No, it just surprised me. Keep going."

My dick slowly slid into his channel. "Relax and it will open up for me, then I can push in deeper. Breathe in through your nose." He sucked in a deep breath and I pushed in. Oh fuck, I was balls deep.

"It might sting for a minute. I'll stop so you can adjust."

"Fuck me now. Please. You don't need to stop. I like the sensation."

"Fuck, alright."

My cock glided in and out of my best friend's ass. I no longer considered him to be my best friend. There was so much more to our relationship than that. Not only was he my best friend, but he was also my lover.

The sound of our bodies slapping echoed throughout the room. Porn was not as good as the real sound! Also, I loved hearing us moan and my headboard tap against the wall.

I watched Alex's reactions as I fucked him deep, hard and slowly. As I dragged my dick in and out of his ass, I watched his little pink flesh quiver. The feeling of fucking his ass was amazing. Unlike anything you've ever imagined. It was better than any porn I'd ever seen. It didn't matter how hard I tried to delay it, I would cum soon.

I grabbed Alex's hips and sides. I needed to fuck him at a different angle so I could drag my shaft over his prostate. Once I found his sweet spot, I knew.

"Holy f-fuck. What. The. Fuck. Is. That?" He asked each word between the thrusts of my cock. My sweet and naive best friend. Of course he doesn't know.

"Your prostate."

After one final thrust, I was shooting my load deep into his ass. Spurt after spurt filled his void. My claimed territory. Alex grasped my bed sheets and started shooting his load all over his stomach.

"Fuck, I'm coming so hard!" he screamed.

I knew his come-face would be epic: Scrunched eyebrows and red cheeks. Mouth hanging half-open. He's so fucking cute.

"Good babe, come for me."

I felt his little hole quiver around my dick. A steady rope of cum spurted from his girthy dick on his stomach. He probably didn't know that I just milked his prostate. I would have to explain it to him later. I could probably convince him that I was the only man who could make him cum like that. It would be selfish not to tell him the truth. Then again, maybe not... I was selfish and wanted to keep him for myself anyway.

"Holy fuck dude, I've never come so hard before." I pulled my flaccid dick out of his ass. He was a perfectly fucked-out sticky mess! Oh and I did lick him clean before we headed to the shower together. He tasted delicious!

After showering together, I climbed into bed. Alex started getting dressed. I jumped out of bed and grabbed his hand.

"Oh no, no. You're not ghosting on me. Not after we made love like that." He looked at me blankly, which was not unusual for him. It was his 'mask.' I dragged him back to my bed.

"How many times have you slept in my bed?"

"I lost count years ago."

"Perfect! And you'll continue to lose count." I was simply implying this wasn't just one casual fling.

We climbed into bed under my covers. I pulled him into my chest and wrapped my arms around him. He was the perfect little spoon.

"I'm gay, aren't I?" Alex asked in a whisper.

"Yep and I wouldn't want you any other way."

I woke up the next morning with a raging hard-on. Alex groaned as my dick pressed into his back.

"Let me suck your dick," he rasped, "I've wanted to suck you for so long." Yep, he had some pent-up sexual tension. He tore off the blanket and sucked my length into his mouth.

"F-fuck Alex," I rasped. I wouldn't last long. He was sucking my dick like a vacuum cleaner. A warm, wet and very gay vacuum.

I shot ropes of cum into his mouth. I wasn't sure if he'd swallow, but he drank me down.

The end

PENETRATE

Straight to gay erotica

Kyle Rayne

"**F**uck!" I shouted at the huge digital screen in front of us. I was with my co-worker James. We were at the airport and our flight was canceled. We were only here for a business trip.

"Josh, we knew this might happen. It's snowing like crazy. Do you really want to fly in a blizzard?"

"I guess not," I huffed.

"Our company booked us a room. Come on, the Uber is waiting to take us there," James said. We were pushing our wheelie suitcases through the madness of a crowded airport.

"When you said they booked us a room, you mean we have to share?" I shouted because it was so loud.

"Yup, but don't be a dick about it. All of the other hotels were full. Do you see hundreds of people here?"

"Yes," I barked back.

"Well, they get to spend the night on the tile floor in an airport, so be grateful."

He was right. We threw our suit cases in the back of the SUV and it was fucking cold. Like the type of cold that made my nuts and dick shrink up embarrassingly small. Whatever though, it wasn't like anyone was going to see it.

We made it to the hotel and I suppose this wasn't so bad. We were being put up in a big, expensive fancy-looking hotel. The lobby was huge and ornate with a bar and restaurant down the hall. The clerk handed us the keycards and winked at us.

"Enjoy your room," she said.

"Thanks, we certainly will," James coolly said with a wink. He looked at me. "We'll enjoy the room, won't we sweetheart?" he asked me in front of the clerk.

"What the fuck?" I said.

"It's the honeymoon suite," she explained, "it's the most expensive room. That's why it was available. Bye lovebirds." She flirtatiously waved goodbye and I felt my cheeks flush red hot. I stumbled away from the counter and made my way to the elevator.

Ding. The elevator door clicked open.

"Hey man, we might have to sleep in the same bed tonight," James said.

"No way! If there's a couch, it's mine."

He looked at me with his dark eyes and he was so relaxed, like this was no big deal and shrugged. "Suit yourself."

That's the thing about James. He's always been so... mysterious. I'm never clear on his intentions or motives. He's not my boss and I'm not his. We're both at the same paygrade, so it's not like I had a 'boss-fetish.'

We entered the room and damn, it was nice. It had a huge bed and a couch. There was a TV on the wall and an artificial fireplace underneath. Ok, so it was a little romantic. I could see why this was the 'honeymoon suite.' Looking at the bed only made me think of sex...

I shook off the odd thoughts assaulting my imagination as I stripped off my boots and coat. My face and body was hot and I wanted everything off. Admittedly, I was flustered.

I laid down on the couch and fiddled with the remote. James walked out of the bathroom wearing nothing but boxers. I didn't want to be rude and stare. He was just getting comfortable, right? Should I get comfortable like that? Would it be weird if I took my slacks off? Well, I wasn't going to sleep in them and I didn't pack pajamas. I've never been able to sleep with clothes on, even in cold weather. I just slept with an extra blanket. So, off goes the slacks. I folded them neatly and put them in my suitcase.

"Getting comfortable, are we?" James asked like damn Yoda.

"Yeah. You're wearing the same as me."

"I like your briefs," he smirked, "they look comfortable. I pegged you as a plaid old-man style underwear guy. Especially the boxers with holiday patterns."

He was such an infuriating ass! I threw a pillow at him.

"Fuck you dude," I playfully said and he ducked. The pillow hit a lampshade and bounced off. So, it was secured to the night stand.

"We're going to wreck this room," James immaturely laughed. "If you don't chill out."

"Ok."

I tried to keep my eyes at face-level. But I did let my eyes look lower and see what type of boxers he was wearing. He was wearing the longer kind, red color. My eyes stayed longer than they should have on the slit in the front. It was open, just a little. I was looking at the slit, but couldn't see anything. Not that I wanted to see *anything*. I was not trying to see another man's dick.

"Like what you see?" he asked and balled his fists and placed them on his hips. I couldn't get rid of the hot feeling flushing my face. But now it all made sense. The playful banter—it was flirting. He pushed his hips out, accentuating his junk—I couldn't deny there was a bulge. Did I want to see it?

"I..." my voice came out as a deep squeak.

He stepped closer to me and I let my eyes look... Like actually look at the details I was seeing. His shoulders were broad and his pecs were big. His torso was muscular and husky. He wasn't entirely ripped, but the muscle was visibly there. He was just a big dude, much bigger than me. His chest was dusted with dark hair.

Underneath his navel was a trail of dark, curly hair that disappeared into his boxers. Fuck, I was more transfixed than I should be. He was the epitome of a manly-man. Me? I was in decent shape, but I wasn't as massive as James.

"I take that as a 'yes.' You like what you see because you keep staring at me." I looked away, embarrassed.

"F-fuck you," I said and looked down.

"Why, yes please. You've been looking at me a while with curious eyes," James said.

That was it! He pushed me to my limits. I stood up and shoved him on the bed. He's big, like I said. James just *let* me push him down.

"Come on man," I said in a pissed voice, "fight me."

He spread his legs open *wide* and propped himself up on his elbows. "I told you we'd wreck the room. I always knew you were the 'angry-sex' type."

My face was still red hot and he was right, I was angry! But I wasn't going to have sex with him.

"That's it! I've had enough of you!" I jumped on him and pinned his arms down, he was big, he fought me. We were wrestling like crazy, fighting for dominance. The nicely made bed was quickly becoming a rumpled mess.

"I could pin you down if I wanted," James rasped, "but I knew this would get your blood flowing. Is your dick hard yet?"

"Fuck no!"

He groaned. "You're getting me hard."

I was beyond mad.

I was on top of him, our chests touching. My legs were dangling off the side of the bed. I bit down on his neck and I hated to admit, my dick was getting hard. He closed his eyes and tilted his neck to the side and *moaned* when I bit him!

"I wasn't sure what kinks you'd have, but I'll take whatever you give me," James rasped.

I was outraged! "You mother fucker." I wanted to punch him... and kiss him. We were a tangle of limbs caught up in the bed sheets. Now, he was on top of me, pinning my wrists at my sides.

"You want this," he said, with his mouth right in front of mine.

"Ok," I huffed, "it's been a really long time since I've gotten laid. Hence the sexual frustration and anger."

"If you let me take care of you, you'll be so high on after-sex endorphins. You'll smile for a week once I'm through with you," James said. I knew that wasn't dirty talk, it was his sales pitch. My half-erect dick was pressed against his thigh and involuntarily my hips were grinding on him.

He tightly grabbed a handful of my hair and tilted my head to the side. The tingle from getting my hair pulled felt surprisingly good.

"Let me suck your dick," he deeply whispered in my ear. "I'll make you feel so good."

Just hearing the deep purr of his voice in my ear, promising me pleasure made my dick pump up fully.

He started sucking my earlobe to tease me. I wanted his mouth wrapped around my dick like that.

"Fuck, ok," I rasped.

He pulled my boxers off in one swift movement. My dick twitched when he ran his hands down my chest and stomach, to my thighs. He placed his hands on my knees and spread them open obscenely wide.

"That's better," he rasped, "I can see you now. All of you."

I wanted to clamp my legs shut, but I didn't. I just never had anyone spread my legs open before. A chick would never do that.

I let him keep touching me. He cupped my sac with one

hand and grabbed the root of my dick with the other. The next thing I knew, he swallowed my dick. He sucked it right into his mouth and *devoured* me like a starving person. Cock-starved, to be exact.

"Oh my god," I rasped. His mouth was so warm... and wet. The way he worked my crown with his tongue.

I actually liked watching another man suck my dick. There was something inexplicably sexy about it. Watching him made me want to return the favor. He seemed to enjoy sucking my length. Maybe I would like it too.

"Let me suck your dick too," I rasped. He stopped bobbing his head but left my cock in his mouth and looked at me with a questioning glance.

"Lay on your side," I suggested, "we can sixty-nine."

I turned around and saw his boxers covering what I wanted very much to see—his dick and balls. He had a big bulge and naturally, I was intrigued. I pulled his boxers down and he was already sucking my dick again.

"Oh my fucking g-god," I moaned when he deep throated me. I didn't know how much longer I would last.

James was right, he was making me feel so fucking good and I wanted to return the favor. I closed my eyes and sucked his head into my mouth. It was dripping with precum and... surprisingly it tasted good. I moaned on his head and sucked down his length as far as I could go. I didn't know how to deep-throat, yet. I knew when my nuts drew up and tingled, getting ready to fire off, that this wasn't the last time I'd be having sex with a man. Well fuck, up until now, I hadn't known what I was missing.

I felt a hand slide onto my ass cheek and tease my crack. I bucked my hips in surprise.

James spit my cock out and trailed a finger up and down my ass crack. "Just let me touch you there. I won't finger-fuck you, unless you want me too."

"Fuck, ok." It did feel good. He sucked my dick back into his mouth. His finger penetrated my crack and teased my hole, just circling it. Around and around he rubbed and I swear I felt my hole quiver. I felt myself wanting to explore this further. It felt good and James knew so much about erogenous zones. I knew he would blow my mind, if I let him.

I reached back and grabbed his wrist and put his finger where I wanted it—my hole.

"Touch me there," I said with a deep and needy voice.

"Let me get my lube." He stood up and walked naked to the bathroom. Fuck, he had a nice ass. He pulled out a small travel-sized bottle of lube from his shaving kit. I laughed knowing that a tiny bottle of lubricant was riding around next to his floss and toothbrush.

"Came prepared," I teased.

"Always," he said with a wink. He lubed up his finger and laid down next to me.

"Turn around again, I still want to suck your dick," I said. I slurped him back into my mouth. He pressed his finger into my ass, sliding it completely in.

And holy fucking-shit! It felt good. His finger grazed across something inside me, like a pleasure spot. My hips bucked, desperate for him to touch that spot again.

"F-fuck dude, what was that?"

"Your prostate," he said with a smirk, "You like that?"

"Yeah," I rasped deeply. He kept stroking it but I wanted more. "I want-" I trailed off while moaning.

"Tell me baby, I'll give you anything you want," James said. Did I want it? Did I want James to fuck me in the ass? Anal penetration... I would have never dreamed of it... until now.

"I want you inside me," I managed to rasp. He was off the bed like a bolt of lightning and digging through his shaving kit again. He pulled out a condom and ripped it open with his teeth. He rolled it down his hard length and fuck he was big! Not that I had much to compare him too.

He came back to the bed and grabbed me by the ankles and pulled my ass to the edge of the bed. He squirted lube on my ass and pushed some in with his finger.

"I've already stretched you, so you're ready."

"Oh," I shyly said with my cheeks flushing red. There was so much I didn't know about having sex with men.

He grabbed my knees and slung them over his elbows, spreading me obscenely wide.

"Your feet look good up in the air," he chortled.

"Whatever, don't make it weird." He grasped my ankles and gyrated his hips until it was pressed at my hole. My eyes practically rolled back in my head at how *fucking good* it felt.

He pushed in, penetrating my barrier. I was moaning uncontrollably. Actually, who am I kidding? I was mewling like a slut. He was pushing in slowly. To fucking slow.

"Come on man, give it to me."

"Ok then." He slid in balls deep, dragged his dick back out, then slammed it back in.

The sound of our smacking bodies together rang across the room. We were both moaning loud! I loved watching him slide in and out of me. It felt so good, I didn't even stroke my cock. It just kept bouncing on my stomach.

"F-fuck, this is fucking good," I rasped.

"I told you that I'd make you feel good."

"I'm coming!" I shouted. I was cuming so hard that I was seeing stars. My ass clenched around his cock when I started firing off round after round onto my stomach. I wasn't even touching my dick and it surprised the shit outta me that I could cum without stimulation. It's really a thing. Don't believe me? Try it for yourself.

I was wet and sticky. My cum completely soaked my body hair. James tilted his head back and groaned.

"Oh fuck, I'm cuming!" I could feel his cum filling up the condom. It felt fucking amazing.

He pulled out and collapsed on top of me. He crashed his mouth to mind and gave me a mind-blowing ravenous kiss.

"I told you that I'd make you feel good."

"You sure did."

The End

Dear reader,

Thanks for reading!

-Kyle

CPSIA information can be obtained
at www.ICGtesting.com
Printed in the USA
LVHW022329180523
747252LV00007B/492

9 798841 865025